ANGRY WHITE MAN

anonymous

ISBN: 978-1-7357240-0-3

The author bears no ill will and intends no disrespect to people of any sex, race, or creed and has written this story in good faith. As history and psychology show time and again, what is suppressed inevitably emerges in a much uglier form. May this story do its part to shed light on our predicament and save us all from disaster.

In the near future...

Sleepless eyes watch the alarm clock. 5:58... 5:59... 6:00. Relentless beeping fills the room. Tom Mayland kills the alarm and trudges out.

★

In the shower, Tom stands still as water streams down his middle-aged, careworn face.

★

An omelet sizzles in the pan, and Tom turns it over. At the table, Billy, a skinny teen with soulful eyes, the same dark blue as his dad's, pours orange juice into two glasses. "I can't take the suspense," he says.

"You check the mailbox?" asks Tom.

"Like seven billion times."

"I'm sure you got in. You talk about that school so much, their mascot better look out for his job." Tom splits the omelet, slides it onto two plates, and places them on the table. As he sits down, his gaze lingers on a framed photo of a blonde with kind eyes, hanging above an empty chair. He looks down. Swallows hard. Forces himself to eat.

"Did you ask the principal about, you know, the raise?" asks Billy.

Tom hesitates. "Today. I'll do it today."

Billy picks at his omelet. "You really think we can lose this place?"

Tom watches his son for a long moment. "Billy."

The boy looks up.

"We'll be okay," Tom says with all the conviction he can muster.

An American flag hangs limp over the house as Tom's dented Chevy pulls out of the garage and drives off down the street, passing several houses with "Foreclosed" signs.

★

Bumper-to-bumper traffic. Tom stares into space, his face beaded with sweat. Feeling his shirt stick to his skin, he holds his hand over an AC vent. Nothing but hot dust. He tries the switch. No luck. Frowning, he slides down the window.

Gangster rap, hard and angry, booms from a nearby SUV and cuts into Tom's eardrums. He looks at the driver – a young Black man with a shaved head and eyes of onyx glares back. For a tense moment, the two lock eyes. Then Tom faces forward and takes a deep breath, his fists clenching the wheel.

★

Napoleon, Gandhi, and Martin Luther King watch from the walls as Tom speaks to the class. "…The Black Codes were created right after the Civil War. They denied Blacks the right to vote, severely limited their civil rights, and forced them to work on the plantations." As the racially diverse eighth-graders take notes, he continues, "Basically, it was a lot like slavery. Most White Americans at the time believed that Whites are naturally superior to Blacks."

A Black girl with golden hoop earrings raises her hand.

"Tonya?"

"I heard someone say Blacks are dumber than Whites 'cause they have a lower IQ," says the girl. "Is that true?"

Tom pauses and considers. "It's true that Blacks have lower IQs on average, by about fifteen points. And IQ is roughly three quarters genetic. But environment is important too – nutrition, healthcare, education."

The girl takes it in, looks down.

"But remember, Tonya, you're an individual, not a race," he quickly adds. "So I wouldn't worry about other people's IQ."

She blinks, then nods.

Tom resumes his lecture: "The Black Codes lasted until the Reconstruction, only to be replaced by what are known as Jim Crow laws…"

★

Tom approaches the door to the principal's office. He takes a deep breath, composes himself, and knocks.

A velvety female voice answers, "Come in."

He enters and steps past a framed Barack Obama "Hope" poster and across the cushy office to the desk of Principal Selma Mahl, a middle-aged White woman with cornrowed hair. She adjusts her glasses and gives him an unctuous smile. "Good afternoon, Tom. How can I help you today?"

Tom searches for words. "Selma, I was hoping... I wanted to talk to you about my... my situation."

"Of course, Tom. Sit." She motions to the chair in front of the desk.

He sits down and shifts uncomfortably.

She leans in, all ears.

"Selma, I know we haven't always seen eye to eye, but... I've done my best for this place. All these years..." Tom hesitates. "I was hoping... Can I please have a raise?"

Selma eyes him for a long moment, sizing him up. Then leans back. "Now, Tom. *Tom*. You know how tight the budget is, with the bilingual ed program and the diversity center and the new wing."

The knot in his stomach tightens. "You're paying me now what you paid me when I started here."

"You know how the economy is."

"I can't make ends meet."

"Financial issues? I'm sorry. Perfectly normal – happens to the best of us."

After a pause, Tom says, "My son and I... I'm... I'm about to lose our house."

"Well, that's unfortunate."

Tom struggles to get the words out, almost whispers: "Please. I really need this."

Selma gives him a tight-lipped smile and spreads her hands in a "what can *I* do?" gesture. He stares at her. Tension builds. She starts to get nervous. Abruptly he rises, making her flinch, and marches out of the office. She stares after him, then yanks a paper tissue out of the box and wipes her nose.

★

As the sun sets, Tom clutches the wheel, lost in heavy thoughts. He drives past a boarded-up restaurant marred with graffiti, and his eyes linger. He and Kathy had really good linguini there, a lifetime ago. They talked and laughed and made plans…

The fuel gauge pulls him out of his memories. Almost empty. He glances around for a gas station.

Gang graffiti, piles of trash, homeless people… Tom frowns as he drives down the grungy street. Passing a billboard in Spanish, he pulls into a gas station, chooses English on the display, and plunges the nozzle into the gas tank. The gallons and the dollars tick away. Feeling his stomach grumble, he heads toward the gas station store.

He opens the door and leaves the USA behind. All the signs are in Spanish, and a Mexican polka plays on the stereo. He steps down the aisle, glancing at the unfamiliar South American brands. He grabs the first thing he recognizes – a banana.

He places it on the counter and greets the cashier, a stocky Mestizo in a wifebeater, with a quiet "Hello." The surly employee just nods and punches in the numbers. Tom pulls out his wallet and searches for cash. Finding none, he takes out a debit card. "Can I get cash-back, please?"

The cashier just stares at him.

"Cash-back," Tom perseveres. "I'd like to get cash."

"Cash... back?" the cashier says with a strong Honduran accent. "No understand. What you want?"

"I want to... Forget it." Tom pays and walks out.

He stops in his tracks.

A tattooed gang of Mestizo youths circles his Chevy.

He gulps. Steadies himself. Then strides toward his car with as much resolve as he can muster. As he approaches, the teens stare at him insolently and sneer. Avoiding eye contact, Tom brushes past them and gets into the car and immediately locks the doors. Without delay, he starts the engine and drives off. Looking at the shrinking gang in the rearview mirror, he takes a deep breath.

★

Pulling into the garage, Tom kills the engine and exhales, feeling drained. He notices that his hands are trembling. He grips the wheel to steady them.

Trudging into the house, he calls out, "Billy?"

No answer.

He steps into the dark kitchen and flips on the light. Billy sits at the table, looking glum. In front of him lies a rejection letter from Dartmouth College.

Tom sighs. "I'm sorry, Billy."

After a long pause, Billy says, "I tried so hard, dad. I tried– I..." He frowns. "There's this kid in my class. Tyrice. He got in. And his grades are way worse than mine. They took him just 'cause he's Black. And that's not fair, dad. It's not right."

"Billy..."

"Remember when I was nine and you and me and mom were at the pier, watching the fireworks, and I asked you why our country is the best, and you said, 'It's the greatest country in the world because it's the fairest

9

country in the world.' You remember that?"

Tom nods.

"You lied to me." Billy gets up and marches out.

Tom stands alone in the empty kitchen, absorbing what just happened. He looks down and notices a letter from the bank amidst the junk mail on the table. He tears open the envelope. As he reads the letter, dread seeps into his face. He slumps onto the chair.

It's a notice of foreclosure on his home.

Sleepless eyes in the dark. The alarm clock beeps. Tom kills it and forces himself up. He sits on the bed, gathering the strength to face the day.

Traffic. Car horns. Tom stares into space.

★

Tom trudges down the school corridor. Another teacher, a brunette in her thirties, calls out his name and catches up to him.

"Morning, Karen," he says.

"Selma's looking for you," she says. "Said she needs to see you right away. What's that all about?"

"Guess I'm about to find out."

★

"*What is going on?*" demands Selma, looking more disconcerted than Tom has ever seen her. "My phone's been ringing nonstop. The parents are furious. I just got off the phone with Ms. Phelps. She said you were telling the kids that African Americans are stupid and inferior."

"I said no such thing," says Tom.

"What *did* you say?"

After a pause, he says, "I mentioned the IQ gap between Blacks and Whites."

Selma can't believe her ears. "Why would you do that? Why would you say something like that?"

"It's what the tests show."

"But why would you *say* that? Are you insane?"

"A student asked me a question. I gave her an honest answer."

"Why would you– you don't– you just don't talk about that kind of stuff. Not in today's society."

"Do you want me to lie to my students?" he asks.

"Not lie," she says. "Just… omit some things. The more… controversial things. You don't want to make people angry. You don't want them to think you're…" she whispers, "…racist."

"So you want me to omit the truth?"

"Tom, c'mon, you have to understand. Some things are… off-limits."

"It's my job as a teacher to tell my students the truth as best I can," Tom says. "I won't lie to them."

Selma considers this. Makes a decision. "I'm sorry, Tom. I have no choice. This school can't afford a scandal right now. I have to let you go."

★

In his cramped office, Tom tosses his things into a cardboard box. Old papers. Stationary. Books on the history of the West. Picking up a framed photo of his wife, he pauses. Slides his fingers over the cracked glass. Then gently lowers it into the box.

Tom lugs the heavy box down the corridor, past students he'll never teach. Past his classroom. He stops. Peers inside... A substitute teacher, Black and chubby, writes her name on the blackboard. Tom swallows hard. Then leaves the school forever.

★

Tom speeds down the freeway, his skin damp with sweat, a thousand-mile stare in his eyes. Barreling into the fast lane, he cuts off another driver, who gives him a long, loud honk. Tom grits his teeth, his fingers clenching the wheel.

The world around him feels hot and hard and hateful.

He's tried so hard to do the right thing. But it's all been for nothing. He's losing everything that matters.

To dull the pain, he turns on the radio:

"...say this may be the hottest day of the year, and it's only getting hotter–" He switches the station.

"...Dow Jones fell again today following the latest jobs numbers. The unemployment rate rose another point three perce–" He switches the station.

A hip-hop song thumps from the speakers. He switches the station.

"...White people. Nothing ever changes. If you're White, you can get away with anything," says a male voice dripping with anger. "Whites got away with slavery. Whites got away with genocide. If you're White, you can do whatever you want."

Tom's face reddens, his nostrils flaring, his muscles winding tight. He looks at the station's frequency on the display. 107.9 FM.

"And you know why? You wanna know why?" the voice continues. "'Cause Whites still got all the power!"

Tom boils with rage, breathing hard, barely able to

see the road ahead. And then something inside him snaps.

The Chevy swerves, cars dodging and honking all around it.

★

The Chevy barrels toward a low, gray building with an antenna on the roof. Above it, a splashy billboard for KYLX 107.9 FM promises "The Hidden Truth."

The car screeches to a stop.

"…telling it like it is," says the voice on the radio as Tom puts the car in park. "Seeing past the lies, past the fake smiles. This is Reggie Miles. Back in five with the hidden truth." A commercial comes on. Tom opens the glove compartment.

There, under a jumble of papers, lies a handgun, dark and heavy.

He stares at it. Then grabs it and gets out of the car.

Eyes afire, Tom marches into the building and down the corridor, past the framed and signed portraits of radio personalities. He runs into an assistant, a young blonde, who freezes on seeing the gun in his hand.

"Where is he?" Tom asks.

"Wh– who?" stammers the assistant.

"Reggie Miles."

She gulps. "He's… on the air." She glances toward the broadcast booth, and he marches past her.

★

The lights on the console are the only illumination in the windowless, claustrophobic booth where Reggie Miles, a charismatic Black man of thirty-four, rants on the air, eyes ablaze. "…Wake up, my brothers. Nothing ever changes. There's no justice for the Black man. There's never jus–"

Tom bursts in.

Reggie stares in alarm at the angry White man with a gun.

Their eyes meet. A long, tense moment.

"So the White man's come to kill me. To silence the truth. Fucking typical," says Reggie. "Well, go ahead. Go ahead, motherfucker. I'm not afraid."

"I'm not here to kill you," says Tom.

Reggie blinks, glances at Tom's gun. "Then what do you want?"

"Truth," Tom says. "And respect."

"That's why you barge in here with a gun? Oh yeah, real respectful."

"That's right," Tom says. "I'm here to hold you accountable. As an equal. Man to man. And the gun, well, the gun's here to keep it real."

"Alright. Alright," Reggie says. "You wanna keep it real? That's what this show's all about."

Tom looks at the microphones on the desk, the lit "ON AIR" sign. As his predicament sinks in, he feels a twinge of fear.

Reggie smirks. "You really wanna do this?"

Tom steels himself. Nods. "People deserve to know the truth." He glances at the mics. "Give me a microphone."

"A microphone?" says Reggie. "This is an AudioScene ZL-seven omnipositional acoustic chamber. You're inside one big microphone, motherfucker." He flips a switch on the console. With a resonant thrum, arrays of red lights come on all over the walls and ceiling.

Tom looks around at the glowing black-and-red electronic cage.

"The whole world's listening," Reggie says. "Whatcha gonna do now?"

The blonde assistant peeks in, glancing from Reggie to Tom to his gun. Tom faces her. She quickly shuts the door.

She bustles down the corridor to a group of worried workers. "Well?" asks a tall technician.

The assistant pants, wide-eyed. "Call the cops!"

★

Police cruisers race down the freeway, lights flashing, sirens blaring.

★

"...So when is it gonna be enough? When will you be satisfied?" asks Tom. "When are you gonna be grateful?"

"When we have *real* justice," says Reggie. "When we have *real* equality."

"You have them already."

"We have a *tenth* of the wealth Whites have. And twice the joblessness. A quarter of us live in poverty."

"There are plenty of rich Blacks. Athletes, politicians, movie stars. A President, for God's sake."

Reggie smirks. "You gonna drop names now?"

"No, but *you* should," says Tom. "Celebrate their success. Instead of acting like it doesn't exist."

"Not enough. Not nearly enough. The race gap must

be closed."

"Close it then. It's on you. Because all the doors are open to you – *all* of them. And if you don't have the guts or the brains to walk through them, don't blame us.

★

Police cruisers speed toward the radio station and pull in. A SWAT team emerges from its armored truck and hurries into the building, carrying assault rifles. The cops barricade the station, forming a perimeter. Snipers take up positions on the surrounding rooftops.

Captain Ray Vallero, a bulky, imposing man well into middle age, steps out of a cruiser and takes a bite of his danish, dripping jam on the asphalt. His baggy eyes give the KYLX billboard a cynical squint as he snorts and barks an order: "Make sure the perimeter's wide enough to hold back the crowd."

Lieutenant Linda Rawlins, whose close-cropped hair makes her look even tougher than she is, glances at the empty street. "What crowd?"

"There's always a crowd." Grimacing, Ray trudges inside.

★

"…You can't see through your thick cocoon of White privilege," says Reggie. "You have no idea, no fucking idea what it's like to be one of us."

"My 'thick cocoon of White privilege?'" says Tom. "Oh, that's right, we Whites don't succeed through hard work. Instead, wherever we go, clouds part and heavenly manna falls on us just for being White."

"You don't get suspicious looks wherever you go. Bad service. Cabs refusing to pick you up. Women clutching their purses. You don't get pulled over by cops 'cause of the color of your skin."

"You know, sometimes the waiter's just having a bad day. And if you don't like getting pulled over by cops, take it up with the giant horde of muggers, gangsters, and drug dealers giving your people a bad name."

"Most of us are not criminals."

"Can't blame people for being rational. Wanting to be safe. Criminals walk the streets because you refuse to be inconvenienced."

"That's right," says Reggie. "That's why we get passed up for loans. For apartments. For jobs. We're all criminals, right?"

"A *third* of Black men are convicted felons," says Tom. "What exactly do you expect?"

Reggie sneers. "Whites always bragging 'bout how 'color-blind' they are. Fucking bullshit."

"Correct," Tom says. "As long as a Black man is fifteen times more likely to be a thief, nine times more likely to be a rapist, twelve times more likely to be a murderer, there can be no 'color blindness.'"

The SWAT team herds the radio station personnel toward the exit. The workers stare in alarm at the armed and armored cops. The SWAT team's leader, Hector Hernandez, a muscular, intense Mestizo of thirty-seven, keeps things under control: "Please stay calm and proceed to the exit." Once the crowd is out the door, he grabs his walkie-talkie: "Floor clear. Moving into position."

The SWAT team takes up positions along the corridor leading to the broadcast booth, assault rifles at the ready. Hector raises his walkie: "SWAT in position. Subject is contained."

★

Ray and Hector step into a large office with a KYLX logo on the wall and abandoned coffee cups on the desks. All around them, cops rush about, clearing out the office clutter and carrying in surveillance and communications equipment as they set up a makeshift command center.

By the window, bathed in the morning light and seemingly oblivious to the bustling cops, sits a slender, bespectacled young man. He studies Tom's dossier on a tablet while listening to the broadcast through headphones.

Hector sizes him up, leans toward Ray: "That's him? That's the negotiator?"

Ray nods. "The kid's got a voice of silk."

The two come up to the negotiator, who is too caught up in his task to notice. "Uh, Jake," Ray says.

No response.

Ray touches the man's shoulder, startling him. The negotiator rises without taking off his headphones. "Jake Hollen," Ray says, "meet Hector Hernandez, tactical lead and one hell of a poker player." Jake and Hector shake hands.

"So you're the miracle worker who talked down the Stillborough killer?" Hector says.

"Every man has his levers," says Jake.

"So what d'you think," asks Ray, "will we make it home before the playoffs?"

Jake picks up the tablet, his eyes lingering on a smiling photo of Katherine Mayland. "The hostage-taker's wife died eight months ago. Shot in a mugging."

Ray frowns at the dossier. "Was the perp…?"

"Shaun Wollins, twenty-four," Jake says. "African American."

"Fucking great."

"Mayland's been in heavy debt after her operations and the funeral. And just got fired over some classroom blunder."

"Just another loser with something to prove."

Jake's eyes run over the dossier, and he rubs his chin. "No priors. No complaints. Graduated summa cum laude. Teaching commendations. The man's a model citizen."

Ray sneers. "A model citizen with a gun and a hostage."

Jake puts down the tablet. Gives Ray a slight smile. "Give me twenty minutes."

Ray smiles back. "Whenever you're ready, maestro."

Jake puts on his earpiece. He loosens his jaw, does a few vocal exercises, and composes himself. He closes his eyes and takes a deep breath. Then reaches for the phone.

"And Jake?"

Jake looks up.

"They're on the air," Ray says. "Make us look good."

★

"...Equal rights – that's all we owe you," says Tom. "And you already have more than that."

"Then where is it?" asks Reggie. "Where is all this wonderful equality?"

"Equal opportunity's on us, but equal outcome is on you. And you don't get to–"

A red light flickers by the phone on the console. Tom stares at it. It keeps flashing. He wavers. Then nods to Reggie.

Reggie picks up the phone. "Reggie Miles here."

"Mr. Miles, you alright?" asks Jake. "Are you hurt in any way?"

"Doing just fine. This is gonna be my best show of the year."

"Good. Can I speak with Mr. Mayland?"

Reggie offers Tom the phone. "It's for you."

Tom takes it.

"Mr. Mayland?" asks Jake.

After a pause, Tom answers. "I'm here."

"Good morning." Jake's voice is calm, almost friendly. "I'm Lieutenant Jake Hollen with the Milton Police Department. I was told that you're in there with Mr. Miles and that you have a gun. Is that correct, sir?"

"That's right."

"Mr. Mayland, may I ask, what are your intentions?"

"Truth and respect."

"Uh, what do you mean, sir?" Jake asks.

"You asked what my intentions are," Tom says. "Truth and respect."

"Truth about what, Mr. Mayland?"

"About what's going on in this country."

"I see," Jake says. "The pursuit of truth is certainly a noble endeavor, Mr. Mayland. And surely you realize this is not the right way to go about it. How can you seek truth with a gun in your hand? What do you say you put it down and come out here, so we can talk about it?"

Tom tenses. A silent pause.

"Mr. Mayland, you sound like an intelligent person. You must understand this is a mistake."

Tom glares into space. Looks at Reggie. Wavers. Decides. "I'm not leaving till I get what I came for."

Ray and Hector, listening in on the exchange, share a look.

"Sir, we just want to make sure everyone goes home safe," says Jake.

"Just leave me alone," says Tom. "Stay out of this."

"Mr. Mayland–"

Tom hangs up.

Jake clicks off his earpiece, thinking to himself. He looks up to see Ray peering at him with an acerbic smile: "What was it about twenty minutes?"

"Let's try again in ten," Jake says. After a moment, he asks, "Do we have his son?"

"Gonna confirm his location and send a unit to pick him up."

"Any intel from the residence?"

"My boys are on their way right now."

★

A police truck pulls up to Tom's house, and armed and armored cops hurry to the front door.

"Police department – open the door!"

No answer.

At the leader's signal, two men ram the door, sending it crashing off the hinges. The cops rush in, guns aimed.

But the house is empty.

They scour the place, room by room, shelf by shelf, closet by closet.

In Billy's room, two cops look over the textbooks on the desk and the sci-fi movie posters on the walls.

In the kitchen, a female cop rummages through the trash and smooths out the crumpled foreclosure notice.

A burly cop barges into Tom's bedroom and sees books and journals on crime, race, economics. He ransacks the shelves, sending the books tumbling to the floor. A photo of a smiling young couple catches his eye, and he picks up the splayed-out journal – a detailed report on the Knoxville Horror and the Wichita Massacre.

★

The cops guard the barricades around the KYLX radio station as onlookers begin to gather, trickling toward the building from all sides.

★

Headphones on, Ray and Jake stand by the phone and listen to the broadcast. Behind them, other cops do the same. "So what's the plan, silver tongue?" Ray asks. "How do we end this?"

"Give him time," Jake says. "Let him talk himself down. The guy's been through a lot. He'll rant, vent, and surrender."

"What if he ends the rant by killing the hostage?"

"I don't think so. He just wants to be heard. The man's not a killer."

"No one's a killer till they kill."

"Let's just take it nice and easy, and no one will die today."

"How do you know?" Ray asks.

"Training and experience," Jake says. "And my gut."

"So you're sure?"

"I estimate a probability of ninety-five percent."

"But you don't *know* know?"

"Not with absolute certainty."

"Then let's just cut transmission."

Jake shakes his head.

"Without the soapbox, he's got no reason to keep this going," Ray says. "He got no audience, he got nothing."

"No, no, you don't take the last scrap of food from a starving dog," says Jake. "Right now, that 'On Air' sign is his whole future."

★

"...When are Blacks gonna stop pushing for special privileges?" asks Tom. "You can't be equal and special at the same time."

"Special? We don't wanna be special," says Reggie. "Just want a fair chance."

"Does your son deserve to go to a good school more than my son because he's Black?"

"Maybe my daughter deserves to go to a good school 'cause when she gets out and starts sending out her resume – and all them bosses see on that piece of paper that her name is Taisha and not Jane, she won't even get half the interviews."

"Bullshit. Every corporation, every government agency is stumbling over itself to hire Blacks. Doesn't even matter anymore if the White guy is better."

"The game's been stacked against us from the start. It's about time you get a taste of your own poison."

Tom shakes his head. "You think this is good for your daughter? For your people? Punishing strangers who never did you any harm."

"They're responsible – you're *all* responsible," says Reggie. "Least you can do is hire a Black kid."

"Who would you want working for you," Tom asks, "the Black kid who got into a great school because he's Black or the White kid who got into a good school because he's smart?"

★

Headphones on, Jake listens intently to the broadcast, jotting down notes on his tablet. Ray rubs his neck and watches him. Jake looks up. Ray raises his eyebrows in a silent question. Jake nods. Then reaches for the phone.

★

"...If all men are created equal, then all racial preferences are illegal," says Tom. "Unconstitutional."

"Racial preferences?" asks Reggie. "You mean, affirmative action?"

"'Affirmative action,'" Tom scoffs. "The only thing it affirms is that racism is good – as long as it's directed at Whites."

He notices that the phone light is flashing red and tenses up. After several seconds, he picks up the phone.

"Mr. Mayland?" asks Jake. "Can we please talk for a moment?"

After a pause, Tom answers. "Alright."

"Think about your son. How do you think Billy's gonna feel when he finds out?"

"This is *for* Billy. For all our children."

"I think I understand what you're doing," Jake says. "White people deserve justice. We need people like you to stand up for our rights."

Ray looks at him, his bushy eyebrows creasing.

"You're absolutely right to bring these issues into the public eye," Jake says. "And that's exactly why right now is the perfect time to end this."

Tom listens, his expression unreadable.

"You've made your point. Very eloquently, I might add. Quit while you're ahead," Jake says. "I think there's a good chance you can get your job back. Sounds to me like a simple misunderstanding."

"Right," Tom says.

"Or you can always find another one. Tens of thousands of schools out there," Jake says. "The important thing is, keep teaching. Pass on your ideas. You don't need a gun for that. What do you say, Tom, if I may call you Tom?"

Tom considers. His lips curl into a mild smirk. "That's very clever, Jake. Very smooth. I bet you're one smart cookie. But not quite as smart as you think you are. And I'm not in the mood for condescension." He slams down the phone.

Jake blinks. Ray watches him, a hint of scorn in his eyes. Jake gulps. Thinks intently. Dials again.

As Tom faces Reggie, the phone light flashes again. Annoyed, he reluctantly picks up. "What, you want to try more tricks?"

"Tom, I'm sorry," Jake says. "I didn't mean to... condescend."

Ray cocks his head in surprise.

"I want to figure this thing out. Give me a chance. No tricks," Jake says. "You want truth and respect? You'll get both from me."

Tom thinks for a long moment. "Alright. Fair enough." He turns to Reggie. "Put him on the air."

"Wh– what are you doing?!" asks the surprised Jake.

Reggie stares at Tom. Tom nods. Reggie shrugs and flips a few switches on the console: "This show just keeps getting better and better."

"If there are no tricks," Tom says, "then we have nothing to hide."

Jake shuts his eyes for a moment. Absorbs and accepts his predicament. Then opens them again. "I agree," he says amiably. "Now, how can we get you to put down that gun and come out?"

Tom searches for words. "My people... we're– we're in terrible danger. We need to... I need to warn them."

"Warn them of what?"

"We're losing... we're losing everything. Our land. Our culture. Our liberty."

Reggie shakes his head, smirking.

Tom faces him. "We're so afraid to step on anyone's toes, so afraid to stand up for ourselves, we're giving up our own future. Our children's future."

"I see," says Jake.

Tom blinks. "You don't believe me..."

"I believe that you believe."

"Leftist, aren't you?"

"I'm... maybe a bit left of center," Jake confesses.

"What do you *really* think, Jake?"

After a pause, Jake says, "I think… what you're saying is a little… dramatic."

"Is it?" Tom asks. "Our borders are a joke. The government works against us. The media covers up Black and Mestizo crime. What they do to us…"

Jake frowns.

"Who speaks for us, Jake?"

"There are plenty of White politicians."

"White on the outside. Democrats speak for the minorities. Republicans speak for the corporations. But who speaks for White Americans?" Tom asks. "They have NAACP, SPLC, NCLR, ACLU, and the rest of the alphabet soup. But who stands up for us?"

Crossing his arms, Reggie shakes his head.

Tom looks at him. "Blacks, Mestizos – they celebrate their race. Take pride in it. They call each other 'brother' and 'sister.' They speak of 'La Raza.' But God help you if you take pride in being White. Right away, you're a White supremacist, a racist, a monster. An outcast."

"Tom–" Jake begins, but Tom interrupts:

"When did it become wrong to care about White people? How did we become second-class citizens in our own country?"

"Why does it have to be about race?" Jake asks. "Must it always be 'us versus them?' I mean, we're all human, aren't we? Race is just a– an artificial category, a social construction."

"If race means so little, why do they use race to deny us jobs? To deny our kids school admissions?" asks Tom. "They'll take a ghetto thug over a farmer's son."

Jake finds his words. "It's not... There are... historical grievances. Lasting damage from the past."

"Do tens of thousands of years of struggle for survival create an 'artificial category?' Did millions fight and perish for their homeland in the name of a 'social construction?'"

"Those were primitive times," Jake says. "We're– we're beyond that now. Beyond tribal thinking."

"Our tribes are what makes us human," says Tom. "Tribes are extended families. And your race is the biggest tribe you can have, your largest extended family."

"The whole world is my extended family."

"'The whole world' doesn't give a damn about you. 'The whole world' hates you for having more than they have – and will kill you for it."

"It's the twenty-first century. The whole world is online. Eating McDonald's and drinking Starbucks," says Jake. "We're exploring Mars, for goodness' sake. It's about time we get beyond race."

"We've gotten so 'open-minded,' so 'civilized,' we can't even see how vulnerable we are," says Tom. "Marching happily toward the cliff with our eyes shut. Everyone else is clawing for power – and we're 'celebrating diversity.'"

"Isn't that the heart of America? All men created equal. Life, liberty, opportunity for all. Isn't that what our Founding Fathers said?"

"Have you actually read what they said? The Founding Fathers, all our heroes, and just about every American before the sixties would be horrified to see what their country has become. They believed in Manifest Destiny – a White civilization."

"And you think that's right?" asks Jake. "We should go back to the colonial days, slavery and genocide and all that?"

"Jesus, I'm not a Nazi," says Tom. "All people deserve decency and respect, whatever their race. But it's one thing to treat people with respect and a whole other thing to hand over your country to them!"

Light filters in through the dusty air, illuminating runes, a Celtic cross, and a Confederate flag on the walls. Rough-edged White youths play pool and drink beer at the basement bar.

The stairs creak as nineteen-year-old Colton Dane marches down them and drops a black duffel bag onto the pool table, scattering the balls.

One of the players, a redhead named Travis, protests: "What the fuck, man?!"

"When they come for you, for your family, you gonna fight 'em off with your cue stick?" asks Colton with intensity that belies his age.

Travis turns away and grumbles sarcastically, "Yeah, I'm sure they'll be here any second."

"No one's making you go," says Colton. "You don't wanna be prepared, it's your choice. It's only your family, your people, your country."

Travis puts down the cue, giving in. "We're getting ready."

Colton looks around, frustrated by his crew's lackadaisical, half-drunken state. "Yeah, I can see that."

He grabs the empty beer bottles and stuffs them into the duffel bag, next to a large-caliber pistol and a sawed-off shotgun.

Seeing the weapons, the boys get serious and gather their things.

Footsteps pound down the stairs, and in rushes Smiley, the youngest of the gang at his baby-faced sixteen. "Hey, guys, you're not gonna believe this!" He flips on the radio. Turns it up. Tom's voice fills the basement:

"...Can't you see? The pendulum has swung too far. We must... we must stand up for ourselves. For our people, for… Christians, Jews, atheists, it doesn't matter – we're all White Americans. We have to work together. Protect our country…"

Colton takes it in, caught up in Tom's fervor. Turns to Smiley: "Who is he?"

"Some teacher who got fired," Smiley says.

The radio goes dead. Otto – twenty, tattoos, shaved head – steps away from it, downs his Budweiser, and slams the bottle down on the counter. "He's inviting the fucking Jews into the White race. Fucking Jew-lover."

"I wanna hear it," Colton says and steps toward the radio.

Otto blocks his way. "Why? You a Jew-lover too?"

The other boys turn to look at the two.

Colton takes a deep breath. Then steps over to the bar, grabs a beer, and takes a swallow. "When I was a kid, when all that shit with my parents was going down, there was this girl at school. Rachel. Skin like silk. Big brown eyes. Real smart. She was the only one who noticed. Who gave a fuck." He takes another swig. "She wore this star with six points on her neck. I didn't know what the hell it meant. And by the time I found out... I didn't give a fuck."

"Yeah?" says Otto. "Well, that don't make the Jews White."

"Yeah, well, since you're such an expert in genetics," says Colton, "what the fuck are they?"

"They're... they're their own thing. They're the fucking Juden."

"I don't know. They look White, they act White, they worship the same God. Maybe they're White enough. I say, if they'll stand and fight for the White race, for Western civilization – let 'em stand with us."

"They're the fucking kikes, man. They won't fight for the White race," Otto says. "Kikes don't give a fuck about anyone but kikes."

"Maybe if ignorant shitheads stopped with all the kike shit and shoving swastikas in their faces, then they'd stand with us."

Otto scowls.

"The Jews are the smartest people in the world," Colton says. "All those doctors and lawyers and scientists – they don't wanna see this country get trashed. There's every fucking reason for them to stand with us."

"Don't call me ignorant. I ain't ignorant."

"When was the last time you read something?"

"Hey, fuck you!" Otto takes a menacing step into Colton's personal space.

Colton stands firm, ready for anything, a wild flicker in his eye.

Otto backs off. Looks down at his beer. Mutters, "Fucking Jews."

News vans arrive at the KYLX radio station. Reporters approach the barricades, eager to interview anyone and everyone, as cameramen shoot the building, the cops, and the growing crowd.

★

"…Always the same," says Tom. "Give me, give me, give me. Give us your money. Give us your power. Give us your jobs. Well, we've been giving and giving – and the free lunch counter is now closed."

"The White man won't give a brother anything without a fight," says Reggie.

"The White man has given you trillions without a fight. *Trillions of dollars.* Welfare, health care, food, housing, education, you name it. And we didn't even get a 'thank you' card."

"Just paying back what you owe."

Tom smirks. "Everyone owes you, and everyone's out to get you."

Reggie shakes his head. "Racism's like a rotten onion. Always another slimy, stinking layer. Always about hate for you people."

"For us people? No one, *no one* is more racist than Blacks."

"That's ridiculous."

"Blacks see race in every conflict, no matter how small," says Tom. "Blacks hire Blacks, Blacks rent to Blacks, Blacks vote for Blacks."

Outside the station, Black onlookers listen to their radios, scowling.

"Blacks form Black-only associations for every profession. Black juries set Black criminals free. Blacks work together to push your interests – and screw everyone else," Tom says. "And you call us racist."

"We do what we have to do to survive in a system stacked against us," says Reggie. "A White system that keeps us trapped in poverty and prison. That fills our streets with despair, disease, and death."

"We don't force-feed you crack. Don't make your kids drop out of school. We don't make your sons join a gang. Don't force your daughters to get knocked up at fifteen."

"You just stand by and let it happen."

"We give you every chance, every opportunity to succeed. More than we get. The government stacks the system in your favor every way it can."

"Racism's got no cure – and we're fighting a global epidemic. For some of us, gangs are the only family we got.

"Does it ever get old?" Tom asks. "Nursing your grievances. Polishing your victim badge. Trying to make us feel guilty for all your failures."

"That's just…"

"Racist?" Tom asks sardonically.

"Offensive."

"My words offend you? I'm sorry. You know what offends me?" says Tom. "A million Black-on-White robberies, assaults, rapes, murders – every goddamn year!"

★

It's lunchtime, and the Milton high school cafeteria bustles with munching and a hundred conversations.

At the Black kids' table, the boys banter and throw glances at the girls, who in turn make eyes at the boys, giggle, and whisper to each other. André Quinzell, big

47

for eighteen, with a bony face, dominates the conversation.

"I'm telling you, man," one of the boys says. "I fucked her in both holes. *Twice*."

"Shut the fuck up," says André. "You don't know what the fuck you talkin' 'bout. You be a virgin 'til your pubes turn white."

Zero, a spry, skinny sixteen-year-old, sits down with his tray, pulls an earphone out of his ear, and offers it to André. "André, check this out."

"Get that shit outta my face."

"Just listen," Zero insists, "you won't believe this shit!"

André reluctantly takes the earphone, puts it in, and listens.

Clam Face, a fat kid with bleach-blond cornrows, speaks up: "Yo, can I hear?"

"Shh!" says André. He listens intently. Scowls.

"What does this mean?" Zero asks.

André thinks for a moment. "My grandpa used to say that one day there's gonna be a war between us and the

Whites. I used to laugh at his ass, but maybe the old nigger was right."

★

Jake looks at the restless crowd at the barricades and speaks into his earpiece: "Tom, I'm wondering if you could be more specific in your demands?"

"You know my demands," Tom says.

"Yes, truth and respect, I remember. But what exactly did you mean by 'respect?' How were you... disrespected?"

"We're all disrespected."

"In what way?"

"Graffiti on our streets is disrespect. Using the government against us is disrespect. Invading our country, stealing our jobs is disrespect."

"I... What are you... what are you trying to do?" Jake asks. "I mean... all you're doing is making people angry."

"It's about damn time!" says Tom. "It's about time

we stop giving up our land, our power. Letting them corrupt our law, rewrite our history, poison our culture."

Jake pauses. "So what can I do, Tom?"

"What *can* you do?"

"What would you like me to do, so we can end this peacefully?"

"Alright," Tom says. "You want demands? Here's my first demand: go take a good look at your badge and think about your duty to your people." He slams down the phone.

★

Tom steps away from the phone and glares into space, gripping his gun.

Reggie watches him intently. "You got fired?"

Tom looks up. "What?"

"The cop, that's what he said before: you got fired."

A pause. "Yeah," Tom says flatly.

"Why?"

Tom faces him. "I gave an honest answer to an honest question"

"What question?"

"Whether Blacks have lower IQ."

"Is that what you think? Blacks are stupider than Whites?"

"It's not what I think. It's what the tests show."

"Measure a Black man with a White man's test, no wonder he don't measure up."

"Bullshit," Tom says. "If the tests are so biased, why do Blacks score lower than immigrants – from a whole other country? Why do Asians score higher than Whites?"

"Guess you're not the smartest bunch around," smirks Reggie. "You go tell all them White supremacists out there. They gonna love that."

"Not the smartest, no," Tom says. "But smarter than you."

"Fucking bullshit."

"No bullshit," Tom says and grudgingly adds, "I'm sorry."

Reggie thinks for a moment, frowning. "On average?"

"That's right."

"By how much?"

"About fifteen points."

A pause. Then Reggie says, "You know what that means, right?"

"What?"

"Even if you're right," Reggie says, "there's a shitload of Black folks smarter than your average White guy."

"True," says Tom.

"How many?" Reggie asks. "How many Blacks above the White average?"

"Around fifteen percent. One in seven."

"That's a lot of people."

"If you say so."

Reggie glowers, leans in. "Does it please you, the IQ gap? Make you feel all warm and tingly inside?"

Tom scowls. "That's right. Do you tingle about all those Black athletes on the pro teams? Hardly a White face in the whole of NBA and NFL." He smirks darkly. "Where's 'affirmative action' when you need it?"

★

A black Cadillac stops near the radio station. Five of Reggie's hardcore fans – all young, Black, male, and edgy – get out and march to the barricades. The cops block their way. The group stays close, glaring at the cops and peering into the windows. Watching them, Linda reaches for her police radio: "This is Rawlins. Requesting more units on the scene."

★

"...IQ is not destiny," says Reggie. "It's just one test."

"On average, Black kids score at the bottom on all the tests," says Tom. "They get the lowest grades. Many drop out."

"Give us good schools, good teachers, and our kids will do as good as your kids. Or better."

"We already spend more on Black students than White ones. We've poured trillions into that black hole. And the gap's as wide as ever," Tom says. "What more do you want?"

"Whatever it takes," says Reggie. "However much it takes to make our schools good schools."

"You think it's just about money? Rich Black kids do worse than poor White kids."

"Whites have better schools."

"You know what makes a good school?" says Tom. "Smart kids. Hell, if a student wants to learn, I would– any teacher would bend over backwards to help. If they really want to learn. And that's not something you can buy."

Ray lumbers across the command center to Mike Voilovsky, a small, taut man with frizzy hair, who is unpacking cameras, cables, microphones, and other high-tech surveillance equipment. "Mikey, where are my eyes?" Ray asks.

A cable camera in his hand, Mike gestures toward the detailed floor map and specification manuals on the table: "It's a soundproof booth. No windows, no infiltration points, nothing."

"Is there AC? Ventilation?" asks Ray. "They gotta breathe somehow."

"It's a custom job – multilayer microcirculation AC. Really beautiful hardware actually. Sound reception and filtration on this thing – unbelievable."

"That's great, Mikey. How do we get inside?"

"We'd have to drill."

"Will the hostage-taker hear it?"

"Everyone will hear it."

"Fucking great," says Ray.

"We can kill the AC," Mike says. "That booth will get real toasty real fast."

"I got a feeling our boy-wonder negotiator would throw a hissy fit."

"So you don't want to cut the power?" Mike asks.

"Can we stop broadcasting without the HT knowing?"

"That's a hard one. Radio waves are everywhere. If we stop it or switch it or jam it, all he needs to do to find out is… tune in."

Ray sighs and shakes his head.

★

More of Reggie's fans, almost all Black, show up at the barricades, listening to the broadcast through portable players and smartphones. A man turns up a radio for everyone to hear.

★

"…*Ninety percent* of interracial crime between Whites and Blacks – is committed by Blacks," says Tom.

"Yeah? What about all the brothers killed by White cops?" demands Reggie.

"We don't kill you. You kill each other. Nine out of ten Black murder victims – are killed by Blacks."

The phone light flashes red.

"Better get that," says Reggie. "Looks like it's time for another hostage negotiation segment of our show." He adjusts a few dials on the console. Offers Tom an earpiece.

Tom grimaces. Then takes it, slides it into his ear, and answers: "Have you thought about it, what your badge means?"

"Yes, Tom," says Jake. "I've been trying to serve and protect you and Reggie all morning. I'm doing my duty."

"Your duty is beyond me and Reggie. Your duty is to the people. Especially your own people. And your people are in deep shit."

"C'mon, things aren't all bad."

"We're in debt up to our follicles. International corporations exporting our jobs from above, illegals stealing them from below," says Tom. "And what's left keeps getting diversified, downgraded, and downsized."

"Last time I checked," says Jake, "most White folks still have jobs."

"Yeah," says Tom, "slaving away months out of the year just to pay for the beast in Washington and all our wonderful 'diversity.' For millions of criminals and welfare mongers. Who abandon their children. Who rob and rape and murder each other – and us. And then call us racist."

"That's– that's just…"

"What? Thoughtcrime? Heresy? You want to burn me at the stake, Jake?"

"You're lucky I forgot my lighter," Jake says. "And that's just not fair. Most of these people, they work hard for their bread. 'Diversity' doesn't mean what you think it means."

"What does it mean?"

"It means… people of different races, different cultures living together, working together. For the common good."

"It's a noble idea…" says Tom. "Too bad it doesn't work."

"It… *can* work."

"It's a myth, Jake. Like the unicorn."

"What makes you so sure?"

"The races are different," Tom says plainly.

"And your race is better?"

"Just different."

"We're *all* different."

"Different races value different things," says Tom. "They don't trust each other. And don't much like each other."

"Actually," says Jake, "there are African and Hispanic Americans I'm very fond of."

"Me too," Tom says. "But that means little next to the Rodney King riots. Or the bloody war between the Black and Mestizo gangs in California."

"There hasn't been an all-out race war yet."

"No," Tom says. "Not yet."

"I don't share your pessimism, Tom."

"You don't share my willingness to accept reality."

"The races *do* work together. We have Black cops, Latino cops, Asian cops, gay cops."

"Gay is not a race."

"Right," Jake concurs.

"We work together because the government forces us to," says Tom. "But we don't live together, don't play together, don't pray together. Except in commercials."

"Maybe that's because of people who think like you."

"It's because we don't want to. No matter what race. In our bones, we'd all rather stick to our own."

"You're living in the past, Tom. The Civil Rights Movement changed everything."

"The Civil Rights Movement is dead. Went from 'equal rights for all' to 'fuck whitey.' All that's left is a twisted cult of race hustlers."

"Like you said, Tom, the world's changing. It's a global marketplace," Jake says. "If we don't learn to deal with all kinds of people, how can we even compete?"

Squinting, his head cocked, Ray watches Jake.

"So we need more diversity, so we can handle more diversity?" asks Tom.

"Something like that."

"Tell that to the Japanese. Japan's as un-diverse as it gets, and they're doing just fine in the 'global marketplace.' And they don't have the problems we have."

Jake sighs, a sad smile on his face. "If only people gave

it a real chance..."

"We gave it a real chance. We gave it *half a century*," says Tom. "And we can no longer afford this disaster, this poisoned myth. Our welfare rolls and prisons are bursting with diversity. And the country's coming apart."

"So diversity's the worst thing since Hitler?" Jake asks sardonically.

"Diversity... is like spice. A little goes a long way. You pour in this much, and the melting pot shatters."

Jake takes a deep breath. "It's not perfect. I know there's a lot of... problems. But it's... the idea. *The first universal nation*. The greatest social experiment of all time."

"I don't want to live in a social experiment," says Tom. "I want to live in a real nation! The real America that our fathers built. And that's dying before our eyes."

★

A "Viva La Raza" flag and "Chicano Power" posters hang on the walls of the cluttered bedroom. Under them, in the battered armchair lounges one of the Mestizo youths that scared Tom at the gas station: a fiery, wiry nineteen, Tiago Morasca talks on his cell phone, his feet resting on the desk. "...She did what? Fuck, I didn't know it can stretch that wide... Anytime, holmes. How much you want?... You got it. Ay te wacho." He hangs up.

He places a handful of cocaine on a small scale. Carefully weighs it, putting some back. Scribbles a record in a ratty notebook. Sensing something, he suddenly looks up.

A short, careworn woman stands in the doorway, staring in dismay.

"Fucking knock." Tiago frowns and seals the drug in a plastic baggie.

In her Mexican-accented English, the woman asks, "Is this what you do instead of school?"

After a long moment, Tiago grudgingly looks up at her.

"We didn't bring you here for this," she says.

"Just 'cause you fuck my dad don't mean you get to tell me how to live."

"This is shameful."

His jaw set, he finishes packing the coke. "I make more cash in an hour than you do in a week. But if you wanna scrub shit outta toilets all your life, go ahead." Hearing no answer, he looks up.

The woman's brown eyes are wet with tears.

He tenses. Gulps. "Fuck this shit." He shoves the coke into a backpack and marches out past her.

Looking glum, Tiago marches out of the graffiti-stained tenement and past an even more graffitied trash bin spilling over with garbage. He kicks a trash bag on the ground, scattering fish bones and chili. Glaring at his soiled sneaker, he picks up the pace. A narco-rap ringtone plays. Reluctantly, he pulls out his cell phone and answers. "What?... I don't listen to the fucking radio... What gabacho?... I don't have time for this shit. I got merchandise to deliver... Really?" He listens, frowning. "Yeah, alright, I'll be there."

★

"...What happened to us? This is a nightmare. Crime. Disease. Addiction. Everywhere, broken marriages, pregnant teens, kids without a father," says Tom. "Have you seen what's on TV? What passes for normal? Thugs, junkies, cheaters, sluts... We used to have standards. Ideals. A culture of honor and decency."

"I hear you," says Jake.

"You're listening, but you're not hearing."

"Why do you say that, Tom?"

"Because you've been hearing very bad advice all your life," Tom says. "And they got you to believe it."

"What are you talking about?"

"I'm talking about treason! I'm talking about the people on top."

"Wh– where on top?"

"Everywhere – the courts, the schools, the corporations, the media. Smug, self-righteous traitors tearing down everything our fathers fought and died for."

"What exactly–"

"Turning our children against their own race. Against their own people," Tom says. "They've done us more harm than an army of terrorists could ever dream of doing."

"They... see things differently."

"They see what they want to see. Fools. Blind to history. Think they can turn human nature on its head with wishful thinking. Turning our country into multiracial, multicultural, multilingual Tower of Babel."

"I think... they think... they're fighting for equality."

"They're lying to us! Covering up what's happening to our people. What they've done to us. How bad it's gonna get."

"They're expanding 'our people' to all the people."

"At the cost of their own people," says Tom. "Do you want to sacrifice our heritage, our freedom for this utopian equality of everything for everyone?

"Why can't we have both," Jake asks, "freedom *and* equality?"

"Can't have both. Doesn't work that way. History, Jake. Since ancient times, they've been enemies. Freedom creates inequality. Equality destroys freedom. One or the other," Tom says. "Our Founding Fathers chose freedom. Our 'woke' elites have chosen equal, common misery for us all."

Jake thinks for a moment. "What about 'All men are created equal?'"

"Equal in the eyes of the law. As it should be. But that doesn't mean equal in talent, smarts, or drive."

"Maybe the strong should help the weak?" Jake says.

Listening in on their exchange, Ray watches Jake with a quizzical expression.

"Maybe they should," says Tom. "But those who are robbed won't help the robbers. And punishing the hardworking and capable for the sake of the lazy and inept is injustice. And it'll kill our country."

"Well," says Jake, "at least they mean well, these 'elites,' right?"

"Wrong," says Tom. "You think the men behind the curtain actually believe their bullshit? 'Equality' is a weapon of mass destruction. They want the system to crash, so they can step in and take control."

★

More police cruisers arrive at the radio station. The cops take positions at the barricades, keeping the crowd at bay under the glaring sun.

★

In the command center, Ray approaches Jake, frowning. "Jake, what are you doing?"

"Negotiating."

"How's your nice chat with the hostage-taker going? Would you like a cappuccino to sip while you're at it?"

"The HT has a lot of pent-up anger and grief. We're talking years, maybe decades here."

"So?"

"So I'm helping him voice his concerns and grievances in a peaceful manner," Jake says.

"This is peaceful?"

"Compared to the alternative."

"But why– why are you arguing with him?" Ray asks. "Just let him blabber till he's done."

"It's not that simple with this one," Jake says. "This guy, he wants to… He wants to talk. I mean, *really talk*."

"So just tell him what he wants to hear."

Jake shakes his head. "This guy's too sharp. He's taken the game to a whole new level. And if I lose his trust, this will cease to be negotiable."

"So you're gonna… what? Debate him?"

"I'm gonna fulfill my end of the deal," Jake says. "I'll give him honesty and engagement – and he'll put down the gun."

"Fucking Jesus. You're making my head hurt," Ray says. "I'm gonna have a smoke and a donut. Call me if anything happens."

★

A beat-up Pontiac Firebird speeds down an empty road past rocks and barren soil, hurling clouds of dust into the air. Colton drives, with Travis riding shotgun. In the back, Otto sulks, Smiley pops his chewing gum, and a quiet boy named Sam watches the passing scenery. Tom rants on the radio:

"...It's a fundamental human right. A basic human need. *To live with your own people.* And they stole it from us. Divided us. Destroyed our communities because they weren't 'diverse' enough."

Colton absorbs Tom's words, gazing at the road ahead. The Firebird veers off the road and rattles over the rugged ground.

"Can't you see what they've done? They swindled us. Swindled us out of our country!" Tom says. "And they're getting away with it!"

The Firebird pulls up to a burned-out cabin, slabs of concrete and charred planks sticking out at odd angles. The boys exit the car. They glower at the empty gasoline canisters on the ground and the graffiti smeared all over the jagged walls.

"Niggers," says Otto.

Smiley turns to Colton: "Was it yours?"

"My grandpa's," Colton says.

Sam shakes his head.

Travis circles the scorched ruin, squinting in the harsh sun. "No shade for us."

Colton spits in disgust. Yanks the duffel bag with the guns out of the trunk. Slams it shut.

★

His gang around him, André strides down the high school corridor, listening to the radio and getting angrier. Students step out of his way. He almost bumps into Odette, a petite Black girl with a pretty face, also listening to the broadcast, but she ducks out of the way just in time and watches the gang pass by.

At the back of the gang, Clam Face talks on his cell phone: "For real?... For real?... Motherfucker!" He hangs up and scurries up to André: "Yo, André, you ain't gonna believe this!"

"That your face's even fatter than your ass?" André says. "I believe it."

"That White motherfucker you listening to – he got a son who goes to this school."

André stops in his tracks.

"He probably here right now!" Clam Face says.

As André absorbs this, his nostrils flare and his eyes harden.

The chemistry teacher, a mild-mannered Asian woman in her forties, steps past the pairs of students at their lab stations. "Make sure to double-check the acid to base ratio and take notes before and after the experiment. And safety first – so don't take off your goggles." The students assemble their Bunsen burners and mix their chemicals.

Billy looks on as his lab partner Tyrice strains to fit a tube over a gas outlet nozzle on the bench. "That's not where it goes," Billy says flatly, trying hard to forget that Dartmouth accepted this B student at best instead of him.

"Yeah, it is," says Tyrice. "Hold up."

"It's not gonna fit."

"C'mon, man, just let me do it."

"Look, I'm telling you, it isn't gonna work."

"Just get out of the way!"

"Chemistry isn't Dartmouth," says Billy. "You can't make it happen just by being Black."

Tyrice stops. Turns. Glares at Billy. Billy glares back. Tension builds…

"Billy!" Odette bursts into the classroom and rushes toward him, out of breath.

Still fuming, he turns to her and snaps: "What?"

She halts, startled. A moment. Then she offers him her pink player. "Is that *your dad?*"

He stares at her. Takes it. Puts in the earphones. Listens… His eyes go wide.

He staggers past her and toward the door. Tyrice and Odette stare after him. The teacher steps closer: "Billy?"

No response. "Everything alright?" Not hearing her, he rushes out.

Hurrying down the corridor, Billy takes out his cell phone and dials. Breathing heavily, his heart pounding, he waits for an answer… as Tom's cell phone vibrates in his Chevy's cup holder.

Billy hangs up. Picks up the pace. Odette chases after him: "Wait, where you going?"

"To the station."

"You can't," she says. "There are cops everywhere. It's on the news."

He absorbs this. "I need a TV."

"I think there's one in the teachers' lounge."

Billy wheels. Hurries in the opposite direction. Odette follows.

A tall Black man with silver hair and a dignified bearing steps off the staircase in front of them and calls out to Billy. Recognizing Dr. Ricard, the school principal, Billy approaches.

"I need to talk to you," Ricard says.

"Do you have a TV?" asks Billy.

★

White people trickle to the barricades around the KYLX radio station. The Blacks eye them with suspicion and hostility. The Whites share this sentiment and keep together.

★

"...I don't quite see the vast conspiracy," says Jake. "Teaching kids some real history. Teaching them to appreciate people of other races. That doesn't seem like brainwashing to me."

"Do you have children?" asks Tom.

"Two sons."

"Are they in school?"

"The older one is starting first grade."

"What's his name?"

Jake hesitates. "Tyler."

"Do you want them teaching Tyler that he's guilty because he's White? That he doesn't deserve what he has? That his forefathers were exploiters and murderers?"

"I, uh... White people have done a lot of bad things, Tom. We should make amends."

Reggie nods his head in silent agreement.

"We'll be making amends till there are none of us left," Tom says. "Listen to yourself. You're arguing against *your own people*! For what? For the sake of strangers who don't give a damn about us? This is insane. This is their greatest triumph."

"'My own people' come in all colors, Tom."

"Why is it so hard for you to take your own side and be a White man?"

"Maybe it's because I share a dream," Jake says. "A dream of a nation where people are judged not by the color of their skin, but by the content of their character."

"It's a good dream, Jake. I'm right there with you," Tom says. "Can you think of a good way to judge the character of a people? How about crime rates? Do you think theft, rape, and murder are a good measure of character?"

"You can't– you can't judge a whole race... Every man is an individual. Every man deserves– deserves to be judged as an individual."

"Do they judge *us* as individuals? Or do they unite against us? Wake up! They don't share your dream. Their dream is power. Because that's what it all comes down to – a power struggle. And they're winning. Because they got us to embrace our own destruction."

Jake searches for words. "White people... White men... we've done terrible things. Centuries, millennia of war. Torture. Genocide. White men have bombed whole cities full of women and children. We enslaved one people and killed off another."

"White men conquered the land, the sea, and the sky. We cracked the atom and ventured into space. Discovered the elements and the continents. Invented science and unlocked the human genome."

In the command center, Ray listens in, finding himself caught up in Tom's words.

"White men brought democracy into the world and founded this great nation," Tom says. "White men are just about the best club you can be in."

Jake absorbs this, somewhat disconcerted. "Maybe we should start a church and worship our Whiteness?"

"Maybe we should," says Tom, ignoring the sarcasm. "Whatever it takes to fight this new, racial Inquisition. Crushing our pride, our kinship. Spreading guilt and fear. Like AIDS – destroying the immune system, so we can't fight back."

"Immune system? What are you talking about?"

"The bonds between us," says Tom. "The true ties of a tribe. Of a race."

"I don't know... Racial unity?" says Jake. "No offense, but that sounds kind of Nazi-ish."

"Funny how it only sounds Nazi-ish when White people do it."

Jake considers. "I suppose so."

"That's because we've been brainwashed," says Tom. "It's natural and good to care about your own. And it has nothing to do with hate. And everything to do with love."

"It's war. It's fucking war!" In the corner of the high school parking lot, André rants to his gang: "He's shitting on our people. Everything we stand for. Wish I could pop that motherfuckin' racist right now! But we'll have to start with his little-bitch son."

Nick, a slight, open-faced boy, speaks up: "André, wait, hold up."

André glowers at him, annoyed by the interruption.

Nick gathers his courage. "He's just talking. And it's not all bad, what he's saying. Some of it is, you know, right on."

"Oh, is that so, *Nick? Nicky. Nicholas.*"

"Stop saying that."

André stalks toward him. "But that's your name. That's what your mommy and daddy called you. A nice White name. So all them nice White folks would love you and welcome you, so you can be just like them."

"Shut up!"

"Or what? Whatcha gonna do, *Nicky?* You house

nigger. You scrawny-ass faggot. You wanna be friends with *everyone*, don't you, you little fag–"

Nick swings at André, but André evades the punch and grabs Nick's arm. He slams Nick against a car, twisting his arm. Nick cries out, then snarls through gritted teeth: "Fuck you. His son is not him – he's just some White kid who's got nothing to do with it–"

His words are drowned out by a yelp as André twists his arm even harder.

"They all got something to do with it," André says.

★

At the barricades around KYLX, a reporter interviews a bespectacled Black businesswoman as his trusty cameraman shoots and the crowd swarms behind them. "He went in there with a gun. Against an unarmed man. That's what it all comes down to," the woman says. "Just another act of oppression. In a long chain of oppression."

Twenty yards away, another cameraman shoots as another reporter interviews a trio of White college students. "I don't know, I mean– I'm not a racist or anything. And I don't condone violence or anything like that," one of them says. "But it's kind of nice, you know, to have someone speak up for us." The other students nod in agreement.

★

Entering the command center, Ray notices that his fly is unzipped and quickly zips it up. He sees Jake typing on his tablet. Approaches. Stares blankly at the screen. "What is this?" he finally asks.

"Population and crime stats. Federal and state," Jake says. "I'm checking the HT's claims."

"Why bother? He's living in a loony world."

"I wish he were."

"Why? What's the problem?"

"Nothing," Jake says. "I mean... everything he's saying... The guy may be nuts, but his numbers check out."

Rays scoffs. "Then make up some new numbers.

Who gives a shit."

"He has a nose for bullshit," Jake says. "One sniff and it's over."

★

A police helicopter circles overhead, its blades slicing the sweltering air. The cops at the barricades watch the crowd grow and listen to the portable radios blaring the broadcast.

★

"...You don't have moral high ground – you have delusion. And never-ending excuses," says Tom. "But you're sure determined not to let the White man off the hook. Judging us. Judging our country."

"Your country was founded by slave owners. Washington, Jefferson, Madison. Lincoln – the 'Great Emancipator' – wanted to send us all back to Africa," says Reggie. "All those big, shiny statues in Washington.

There's your fucking heroes."

"There you go. A moment of truth. Fuck the Founding Fathers. Fuck America. Let's burn it all down!"

"It's not... it's not like that."

"It's not? Isn't that what you really want in that deepest, darkest part of your heart? The part you won't admit." Tom points to his eyes. "We can see it, Reggie. We can see it in your eyes."

Reggie shakes his head. "You can't enslave a people for two and a half centuries and then just 'set them free' into hostile lands with nothing but the rags on their backs – and expect them to prosper."

"Everyone else did. Every wave of immigrants prospered in a generation. No matter how poor, how ignorant, how unskilled. And they didn't even speak English."

"Man... We had *empires*. Ghana, Mali, Songhai. Vast and rich and powerful. If not for Whites, we could've been kings."

"If not for Whites, you'd be starving in Africa, not raving on the radio" – Tom gestures at the arrays of red lights around them – "from your million-dollar microphone."

★

Headphones on, Jake listens to the broadcast and scribbles notes, thinking to himself. Hector comes up to him. "So what do you think, Jake? We gonna have to shoot this guy?"

"That won't be necessary. The guy's just having a really bad day."

"Too bad he hates everyone except White folks."

"He never said that."

"Didn't have to," says Hector. "You can just tell."

"You can?"

"Why else is a White guy talking about this stuff?"

"Are White guys forbidden to talk about this stuff?"

"You can talk about whatever you want, Jake. It's what you're good at," Hector says. "But just in case that doesn't play out too good, my boys and I will put the fucker down faster than he can shit his pants."

★

The number of Whites at the barricades keeps growing. The White and Black groups keep apart and throw glares at each other.

★

Ray paces across the command center, talking on his cell phone. "Yeah... No... Fucking press. Tell the vultures we got it under control." He frowns as he listens. A subordinate approaches with a quiet "Sir" and offers him another phone.

"Not now."

"It's the Chief."

Ray stares at the phone. Takes it. "Morning, Chief, how you doing?... Uh, sure, Chief, give me a second." He steps out and into an empty office. Shutting the door, he glances around and brings the phone to his ear.

Behind a burnished desk in the heart of the city sits the Chief of Police, his shrewd eyes gleaming amidst the deep creases of his face. "Ray, what the hell's going on down there?"

Ray hesitates, taken aback. "We're working to end the stand-off, Chief."

"Why are you on the air?"

"W– we didn't wanna back the HT into a corner. The negotiator, he thought it was too risky, uh, too dangerous."

The Chief grimaces. "I knew you weren't MENSA material when I promoted you, but this... this is beyond rookie."

"Chief, I did everything by the book. Standard procedure. What was I supposed to do?"

"You were supposed to cut transmission as soon as you set foot there. And now it's too late because the media's already involved."

"I– I acted on the advice of the negotiator. Lieutenant Hollen. He has a very good rep."

"I see," the Chief says. "Who is this Hollen? One of our guys?"

"He's a transfer from Welling."

"Wait… Hollen…" The Chief frowns. "The same Hollen who talked down the Stillborough killer?"

"Yup, one and the same."

The Chief considers for a moment, looking out at the bustling city below. "Ray, this situation, this… predicament – it's very sensitive. And the longer it keeps going, the greater the chance there will be a… misstep."

"Of course," Ray quickly agrees.

"We can't have this turn into a media circus. We need to end this fast. One way or another."

"I'll end the negotiation and prepare to breach."

"No," the Chief says. "There might be casualties. A man with Hollen's reputation has people's ears. He talks, and we end up with a scandal."

"I'll get him on board, Chief."

"You two close?"

"Close enough."

"Then make him understand our predicament. Make him part of the plan. He seems… reasonable."

"Yes, sir."

"I'm counting on you, Ray," the Chief says. "The department's counting on you."

★

On a dusty TV screen, a reporter speaks in front of the KYLX radio station, a crowd roiling behind her: "...The broadcast continues despite the stand-off. And the on-air debate is drawing quite a crowd. The hostage-taker's identity has been confirmed. Tom Mayland, a history teacher at Riley middle school, was fired this morning, following accusations that he made racist comments in the classroom..."

Billy stares at the portable TV, breathing hard and clutching his thighs. Seeing the boy's growing panic, Principal Ricard turns the TV off. Billy keeps staring, ashen.

"Billy, I know it looks bad, but you need to stay calm. The police will sort it out–"

"I have to go." Billy jumps up from his chair.

Ricard rises to stop him: "No. You're not... It's

better if you don't walk around alone right now. Your dad's opening a lot of old wounds."

"I…" Billy begins.

"The police are on their way. They'll take you into custody, so you'll be safe–"

"No! You don't understand," Billy breaks in. "It's my fault. I… I have to stop it." He bolts out of the office. Ricard rushes after him, calling his name. But Billy is already racing up the corridor and down the stairs.

Billy yanks out his cell phone and dials with trembling fingers…

In the school library, a curly-haired junior named Dylan searches a row of books on the American Civil War. His cell phone throbs in his pocket, breaking the quiet. He fishes it out and whispers, "What?"

"I need your car," says Billy. "Right now."

"Can't. I have eighteen minutes left to finish my history paper."

"Dylan, this is beyond emergency. If you're my friend, meet me at the lockers *now*!"

"Fuck. Alright."

Billy hangs up and turns the corner. Moments later, he rushes up to the lockers. He paces, biting his nails. Abruptly he smashes his fist into a locker. His knuckles scratched and bleeding, he winces and slumps against the row of metal boxes, sucking in ragged breaths...

Hearing footsteps, he calls out, "Dylan!" He gets up and steps forward.

In front of him stands a hulking figure wearing a goblin mask. Behind the goblin are others: Black teens in party-store masks – a skull, a chimp, a Chewbacca.

The goblin studies Billy, menace in his dark eyes.

Billy backs away. Trapped between the lockers.

The goblin stalks toward him... "So your daddy starting a war, that it? Well, we ready. We ready, motherfucker."

He slugs Billy in the face, knocking him to the floor.

Billy spits blood and tries to get up.

Behind the mask, André sneers, savoring the rush of power. And then kicks Billy in the head.

The gang surrounds Billy and showers him with kicks...

Dylan hesitantly approaches the ruckus... "Billy?"

A member of the masked gang shoves past him, jolting him. The gang quickly disperses. Dylan stares after them. Then turns and hurries to the lockers.

His eyes widen as he sees Billy, battered and bloody, lying still on the grimy floor.

"Billy!" he cries out and rushes up to his friend. Checks his pulse. Presses his head to Billy's chest and listens for breathing.

He yanks out his cell phone and dials 911, his chest heaving. Waits... Finally the dispatcher comes on. "My friend– he– he's not breathing," Dylan says, his voice breaking.

At the barricades, Linda bullhorns the restless crowd: "Everyone, please stay calm. We're working to end the stand-off as soon as possible."

Someone in the Black throng yells out, "Fuck you, police Barbie!"

Linda takes a deep breath. "Let's just all take it easy, and no one'll have to be arrested."

★

Headphones on, Jake listens to the broadcast. Ray's hand on his shoulder jolts him. "Jake, we gotta talk." Jake takes off the headphones. "In private," Ray adds.

Jake gets up and follows him out and into the empty office.

Ray looks around once more and clears his throat. Jake watches him. "Jake, this whole thing, it's... sensitive. The media's up our asses; reporters and cameras. We gotta look good," Ray says. "Public relations and all that."

"I understand," says Jake.

"Good, I knew you would. You know we can't stretch this out. Careers are at stake here. Speed it up, will you?"

"I'll do my bona fide best to end this as speedily as possible – without jeopardizing the hostage. That's our first priority, right?"

"Of course… I'm just saying, if you have to cut a few corners – cut a few corners."

"There are no corners."

"There aren't?"

"No," Jake says. "Two lives are at stake. And that's a hell of a lot more important than our careers."

Ray rubs his neck and takes a few steps. "Look, I'm just saying, you gotta be mindful of the politics."

"I won't take a second longer than the situation requires."

"It was your idea to do this on the air."

"I stand by my decision. Everyone's still alive."

"People are watching, Jake. Important people," Ray says. "You play your cards right, I see a very bright future for you in this department."

★

Outside KYLX, the crowd keeps growing in size and agitation, Mestizos joining the Whites and the Blacks under the blazing sun.

★

"...Lower wages, higher rents, more traffic, crowded schools – it's a gift that keeps on giving," says Tom. "One race problem wasn't enough. We had to import another. And now a third of Mexico has moved in." He smirks. "Soon we'll have to speak Spanish just to get by."

"We're a nation of immigrants," says Jake. "Always have been."

"Never like this. Immigrants used to respect our laws. Our borders. They worked their ass off, grateful to be here."

"Mestizos work as hard as anybody."

"Mestizos invade our borders. Spit on our laws. Bring drugs and gangs into our streets. Our schools." Tom paces, clutching his gun. "Heroin, fentanyl, meth. Mexican drugs kill *tens of thousands* of Americans – every single year! And that's not counting the *thousands* killed by Mestizo drunk drivers!"

Jake takes this in. Blinks. Finds his words... "All the other immigrants – the Germans, the Irish, the Italians

– they all struggled in the beginning."

"The Germans, the Irish, the Italians – came here to be Americans," says Tom. "These people, they're not our race. They don't want our language. Our 'Anglo' culture. Our values. All they want is our land and our money. This is not immigration – this is an invasion!"

"They're… they're unarmed men, women, families just looking for a better life."

"Unarmed? True, they don't come carrying guns, but they're armed well enough. They carry crime and poverty and disease."

"What disease?" asks Jake, incredulous.

"Chagas disease, tuberculosis, malaria, hepatitis, you name it."

"You want to send sick people away? Punish their children?"

"What about *your* children? Your two sons? What about my son? What about our own families? Our own people?"

"What about them?"

"Are they worthy of your concern? Do they deserve

to be safe? Healthy? To keep what they earn?" Tom asks. "All you noble crusaders always want to save people somewhere else. And never your own."

"We can't just– just kick them out. Send them back to their hellholes," Jake says. "We're a civilized nation. We have to be humane."

"Humanity starts with your own people. There's nothing humane about hurting our own for the sake of strangers who don't give a damn about us. Who demand racial privileges. Who steal our jobs and every year send *tens of billions* to Mexico – and then expect us to feed them and house them, educate them and medicate them for free."

Jake shakes his head. "That's... You don't... Listen, they're just people – they're not monsters."

"No, they're not monsters," Tom says. "They're just people from another tribe – who are taking over our land."

Reggie blinks and frowns, thinking to himself.

"Most of them– most immigrants – are here legally. Fairly. You're a history teacher. Remember the nineteen-sixty-five Immigration Act?" asks Jake. "We *chose* to open our borders."

"How can I forget the greatest mistake in our history? And the biggest lie," says Tom. "They promised us, they swore immigration wouldn't hurt our people."

"Politicians, they…" Jake gropes for words. "I mean, the world's getting smaller and smaller anyway. Do we even need borders anymore? A world without borders sounds pretty good to me."

"A world without borders means say goodbye to your house, your car, and that nice summer vacation you were planning – because ten brown people will gladly do your job for a tenth of your pay."

"You think it's all about money?"

"What else? The banks, the corporations – they don't want to pay American workers American wages. Why, when you can import endless cheap labor from the Third World?" Tom sneers. "Privatize the profits and socialize the costs."

"I'm not sure I understand–"

"We're the suckers paying trillions for Third World strangers – so they can take our jobs. Spoil our culture. And drown out our voices," Tom says. "This is treason! Can't you see?!"

★

Riled up by Tom's words, the crowd pushes against the barricades. The cops stand their ground.

★

Ray and Hector huddle in the command center, watching Jake and listening to the broadcast. Hector scowls, his muscles tense. "You just gonna let him talk?"

"It's what Jake wants," Ray says.

Hector shakes his head. "I don't know. I don't know, man."

"Why, you ready to go in, guns blazing?"

Hector looks up at him. "Just say the word."

★

Tom paces, gun in hand. "…Hundreds of thousands of illegals march on our streets, demanding *our* rights – our children's rights. Threatening us. And we just run away. Flee our streets, our cities, our states. As far from 'diversity' as we can get. Refugees in our own country."

"The illegal… the undocumented, they're… fellow human beings," says Jake. "If they risk so much, want it so badly… we should let them be Americans."

"They're already a separate nation within our borders."

"I don't think you're helping unite the country here."

"What *can* unite us?" Tom asks. "What can hold this country together if we have nothing in common? If we don't speak the same language. Don't read the same books. Don't have the same heroes. Don't see the same right and wrong."

"We watch the same movies. Eat the same pizza. Drink the same Coke. Or Pepsi. We share the same land. Work together. Maybe for now that's enough?"

"A nation is not a piece of land. It's not an economy. Or a bunch of ideas. It's a living thing – a people united. And our nation is dying. Because we don't have anything to unite us anymore. No race. No culture. No morals." Tom smirks sadly. "Except for greed. And you can't build a nation on greed."

★

The school doors burst open, and two paramedics carry the still Billy out on a stretcher. They hurry past the crowd of shocked students and into an ambulance. Dylan stares, not knowing what to do. The ambulance doors shut, and it speeds off, siren wailing. Odette watches it disappear down the street, frowning and biting her lip.

★

The room is a mess. The gang of Mestizo youths from the gas station hangs out and listens as Tom's voice rumbles from the phone in Tiago's clenched fingers:

"...I know– I know that's not most of them, but... A Mestizo is four times more likely than a White to be a murderer. *Nineteen* times more likely to be a gangster. These are hard numbers. We must– we have a responsibility... We must protect our families. We must protect our people!"

Luis, seventeen with dumbbell-pumped biceps and a budding beer gut, gulps down his Corona and rolls the bottle along the floor. As he reaches for another bottle, he leans on Tiago fidgeting on the edge of the couch. Tiago pushes him away: "Get off me, man!"

"Easy, ese. It's all good."

Tiago springs from the couch, towering over him. "You're fucking stupid!" He points to the phone: "The gabachos are getting pissed. And all you're thinking about is your Coronas!"

"Don't call me stupid, cabrón. I'll fuck up any gabacho that fucking looks at me how I don't like."

"You *are* stupid, burro. One gabacho ain't the problem. We can do what we want with any one gabacho. But if this goes bad... If they all get together..."

"Then we get together too," Luis says. "How many gangs out there? How many vatos in each gang? Every one is a soldier."

"The gabachos are loco. They live for war. It's in their blood. That's why they're trying so hard to be nice all the time. If we piss them off, they... they'll come for us."

"Let them come."

"They'll kill us, wey. Kill our fathers. Our mothers. Our little hermanos and hermanas. And they'll come south for our cousins and grandfathers. Chingue a su madre!"

Mateo, a chill burnout of eighteen, slumped in a rocking chair, puffs on his blunt and lets out a cloud of smoke. "They won't come. Not if we don't fuck with them. Did you hear what the man said? They don't wanna kill us. They just wanna be left the fuck alone."

Tiago turns to him. "We gotta be smart. Gotta be prepared. Gotta make alliances. Get our numbers up."

"Who do you wanna make alliances with?" Luis asks.

Tiago thinks… "André."

Luis sits up. "You wanna be homies with the chardos?"

"Make alliances, not homies, fool."

"Why would they make alliances with us?"

"'Cause they're just as outnumbered as we are."

★

Amidst the sunbaked crowd outside KYLX, a reporter interviews a bearded, ponytailed White man who happens to be a college professor. "It's highly irresponsible for these… individuals to be having this sort of conversation on the air. This just demonstrates how it's high time to make hate speech illegal," the professor says. "Yes, yes, I'm well aware of the First Amendment, but this kind of… 'free speech' is very dangerous to the fabric of society."

Thirty yards away, another reporter interviews a middle-aged Black auto mechanic. "I say let them talk.

Doesn't do us any good to hide all this stuff. Just makes things worse. Makes them… fester," the mechanic says. "If we put it out there, maybe we can find some way to deal with it, you know?"

★

"…Our elites, you have to hand it to them – they are relentless," says Tom. "They just keep selling it to us. Schools. Politicians. Hollywood. Shoving it hard down our throats. Their 'diversity.' Just about every textbook. Every policy. Every movie."

"Selling us what exactly?" asks Jake.

"Selling us this myth– this multiracial utopia – where all the minorities are wonderful, and the bad guy's always White."

"They have Black villains. In the movies, I mean."

"When was the last time you saw a truly despicable Black villain?"

Jake thinks… gives up. "Okay, so it's a little… sugarcoated. But they're trying to… help us all get along. Is that really so bad?"

"They're lying to us! Can't you see? They're keeping us in the dark."

"About what?"

"About the genocide of White farmers in Africa. About Islamic terrorism. About the million violent crimes *every year* against our people! Jesus Christ..."

Jake sighs. "They're trying to... trying to focus on the best of it. You want them to focus on the worst?"

"I just want them to tell the truth! Stop brainwashing us. Stop shoving this lie– this poison down our throats!"

"They're telling us... showing us... how the world could be. Should be. That if we can get through this... diversity can be a wonderful thing."

"If it's so wonderful, why do we need constant reminders of how wonderful it is?"

"So we can learn to... appreciate it."

"Wonderful things – are easy to appreciate," Tom says. "If diversity really made our lives better and not worse, it wouldn't need to be sold or managed or 'celebrated.'"

"I think a little celebration can't do any harm."

Tom scoffs. "Woo-hoo! We're passed over for jobs! Yippee! We're losing our land! Hooray! We're gonna be a minority in our own country!"

★

With lights flashing and siren wailing, the ambulance screeches to a stop in front of the hospital doors. The paramedics rush to place Billy on a gurney and wheel him inside.

★

The .44 Magnum looks huge in Smiley's small hands as he aims it at a beer bottle placed on a rock... Boom! He fires, jerking back from the recoil.

The bottle remains unharmed.

He fires again. No luck. "Fuck!"

Colton comes up and adjusts Smiley's stance. "Keep your balance."

Smiley fires again. The bottle bursts, glass shards

gleaming in the bright sun.

"Yeah! That's right!" he exclaims and pumps the air with his gun arm, inadvertently pointing the gun at Colton – who calmly but firmly moves it aside.

"Sorry," Smiley says and wipes his forehead. "Whew. It's fucking scorching. I'm gonna get some water." He carefully hands over the .44 to Colton and tramps off toward the car, passing the charred ruins of the cabin, where Travis and Sam reload their guns while Otto snaps open a Coors Light and takes a swig.

Smiley gulps down his water and looks up at a burnt wall marred with graffiti, shaking his head. He notices a spray can abandoned in the dirt. A pause. Then he picks it up. Shakes it. Sprays over the graffiti…

"FUCK DIVERSITY" in big, bold, red letters.

He is finishing up the "Y" when his cell phone rings. He fishes it out of his pocket and answers. "Hey… When?… Fuck… *Fuck!*"

He rushes over to Colton, who is aiming the .44, his hands steady. Just as Smiley stops and opens his mouth, Colton fires. A beer bottle shatters. He fires again, and another bottle explodes. A third shot, and a small watermelon erupts into red pulp.

Smiley stares for a moment, then gushes: "Derek just called. A Black gang beat up a White kid at his school. Real bad. They're saying he might die."

Colton absorbs this as his startled gang converges. He reloads his gun, slides on his dusty jacket with the Rebel flag on the back, and speaks with icy resolve: "Let's do something about it."

★

Outside KYLX, a young Black man breaks through the barricades and dashes toward the entrance. Linda tackles him to the ground and cuffs him as onlookers shout and push against the barricades.

★

Jake stares at the crumpled foreclosure notice from Tom's house. Ray watches him. "Is he getting to you?"

"No," Jake says. "It's just… new. Nothing to bargain with. He's a… a true believer."

"You actually buying all that crap about saving White people?"

Jake shrugs. "He doesn't want anything from us."

"Everyone wants something."

"Yeah, truth and respect…"

"Christ," Ray says, "instead of you talking him down, he's talking you up!"

"I can handle him, Ray. I'm getting a good grasp on his psychology."

"While you're playing shrink over here, he's talking and talking, and that mob out there is getting bigger and bigger."

"This approach is by far our best chance for a peaceful resolution."

Ray glances around. "Jake… kid, you gotta listen. The stakes are sky-high. The whole department's exposed. Major players are involved. You get my drift?"

"What major players?"

"Don't worry about it. Just wrap it up. Or we might

have to do it for you."

Jake blinks. "Are you– wh– what are you saying, exactly?"

"I'm saying, we gotta put a lid on it. All this blabber on the air is bad for us. Bad for the brass. Bad for me. Bad for you."

"We're just talking. How much damage can we do?

"Christ, you're a fucking boy scout," Ray says. "With race, it's all politics."

"I'm just trying my best to save two lives."

"What you're trying is my patience."

★

"...All these decades," says Tom. "We've tried so hard. Done so much for you..."

"You think it's that simple?" says Reggie. "My people – we were severed at the roots. Torn from our homeland. Stripped of our families, our culture, our history. Our whole memory smelted into White man's gold."

"All the history you want is waiting at your local library."

"You think you can get your soul back from a book? Everything around us celebrates the White man. All your paintings in the museums. All your big-ass statues and monuments. All the streets have White names, and all the schools teach White history."

"People like you have done a great job renaming our streets and rewriting our history."

"At least you have a history. Ours is gone. Drowned in the ocean between here and Africa."

"Schools all over the country teach your history. It even has its own month."

"Fuck your month."

"We even celebrate Martin Luther King's birthday. What the hell has King ever done for us?"

"Taught you to be human."

"We don't need lessons in humanity from a Marxist sex addict who watched a rape and laughed," Tom says.

Reggie shakes his head. "You can't understand."

"Understand what?"

Reggie looks up at him. "We just want you to… to make us whole again."

"Jesus, what more do you want? Should we tear down the Founding Fathers and put up African kings? Burn the museums? Become your slaves? When is it gonna be enough?"

"We lost *everything*. Can you get that? All the precious pieces."

"Yeah, you lost it. But you only lost it when you went chasing after the free lunch."

"Fucking bullshit."

"Gangs and drugs, crime and fatherlessness – all your miseries – all soared after the Civil Rights Act."

"Just more reasons to feel superior, right, Tom?"

Tom peers at Reggie. "Do you like your car?"

"What?"

"Your car? How about your phone – you like your phone? Your computer? The Internet? AC? Radio? All these things you take for granted were created by White men. Art and science and law and philosophy–"

"Don't forget slavery and genocide and nuclear war.

Wouldn't wanna leave those out."

"That's right. That's our history, warts and all. We've done great things – and terrible things. And we've paid for our mistakes," says Tom. "But here, we take pride in our people. And our nation. So stand with us or against us. But save us your whiny, self-righteous bullshit."

As Jake steps down the hallway and past the SWAT team, a Black cop gives him a dirty look. Tensing, Jake enters the command center, bumping into Hector, on his way out. Hector turns to him and jibes: "Hey, Jake, you gonna invite Tom to your next birthday party?"

"What do you mean?" Jake asks.

"Getting real cozy with the HT there."

"It's imperative that he feels I'm on his side."

"Are you? On his side."

"There are no sides," Jake says. "We're here to make sure no one gets hurt. And the odds improve exponentially if the HT doesn't feel trapped and alone."

"Oh, he's definitely not alone," Hector says. "Millions like him out there."

"As many ways to see the world as there are people in it."

"Do you see what he sees?"

"No," Jake says. "But seeing things is not a crime."

Hector twitches. "Whatever you say, amigo."

★

"You're still on the air," says the Chief of Police. "What's going on? Did you speak with Hollen?"

"Yeah," says Ray.

"Well?"

"We're working it out."

"You're working it out?"

"Like you said, Chief, it's real sensitive."

"He gonna be a problem for us?"

"No, Chief. I– I got this."

The Chief taps his fingers on his desk. "Did you

sweeten the deal for him?"

"Yeah."

"And?"

"He didn't bite," Ray says. "He's a goddamn idealist."

"Every idealist has his price."

"The kid's got a stick up his ass."

"Then scare him. Make him fear for his badge."

Ray wrestles with himself for a moment. "He's a good cop, Chief."

"I see you care more about his future than your own," the Chief says. "Maybe I should call *him* instead?"

"Chief, I didn't mean… Look, I'll do it," Ray says. "I was just thinking maybe there's a better way?"

"Only two ways, Ray. Only two ways to make a man do something," the Chief says. "Make him want it. Or make him fear it."

★

"…I'm fed up with the endless parade of sob-stories," says Tom. "*Everything* is White man's fault."

"You think these people are suffering just to guilt-trip you?" asks Jake.

"Can't you see? It's misdirection. A magic trick."

"Misdirection?"

"They're distracting us from what really matters."

"Distracting us? Why?"

"So they can bury all those nasty numbers, all that scary science – anything that threatens their lies."

"Numbers change," says Jake.

"Sure – if you drop all the standards."

"What standards?"

"We had the best schools in the world. Now we're behind Poland," Tom says. "And now they're diversifying the army, so we can have Blacks in charge of nukes." He looks at Reggie, who glares back.

After a moment, Jake asks, "Well, what about Asians?"

"What about them?"

"They're doing better than Whites," Jake says. "Highest education. Lowest crime rates. What more could you ask for?"

"Asians are not the problem."

"So Blacks and Mestizos don't deserve a fair chance?"

"Blacks and Mestizos live better here than anywhere else. But it's not enough for them," Tom says. "And no matter how much they get, it'll never be enough."

"Why is that?"

"Because their 'noble fight for justice and equality' is bullshit. This is about power. Pure and simple," Tom says. "And we're so busy kowtowing and apologizing, we can't even see their shameless power grab."

Reggie stiffens, glowers at him.

"You're making a lot of assumptions about a lot of people here," Jake says. "Maybe you should ask *them* what they want."

"No one asked *us* what we want!" Tom says. "No one asked us if we want 'diversity.' If we want to pay Third World people, so they can breed like rabbits and colonize our land. If we want to give up our schools. If we want strangers from all corners of the world on the streets where our children play."

"Jesus…"

"You're so brainwashed, you can't even think about what I'm saying, can you?"

"I'm thinking."

"Don't you see? We're so afraid, so utterly terrified of being racist, they can take over our country by calling us names."

"It's not… it's not that simple," Jake says.

"It's very simple. Let me tell you what 'diversity' really means."

Jake gulps.

"Diversity is the opposite of community," Tom says. "It means constant suspicion. Countless grievances, accusations, lawsuits. It means political correctness kills free speech – and free thought. It means immigrants don't have to learn our language, embrace our culture, or rise to our standards."

At the barricades, the White throng simmers, taking in Tom's words.

"It means more people who don't play fair. Who demand racial privileges – at our expense."

The Black throng bristles. The Whites and the

Blacks mutter and glare at each other.

"It means more and more people need the government to be their nanny. And the government gets bigger and bigger. And our liberty gets smaller and smaller. And our taxes keep rising to pay for endless poverty and endless crime."

In the command center, Ray listens, frowning.

"Diversity means we're not safe in our own country," Tom says. "And this is what they want us to celebrate."

Jake blinks. "That's… quite a mouthful."

"Not getting through, am I?"

"I'm listening."

"But not hearing."

"Well, do you want me to just blindly accept everything you say?" Jake asks. "I mean, a lot of people would disagree with you."

"I have an idea," Tom says. "Try something radical – try thinking for yourself."

★

The orderlies wheel Billy into the operating room and lift him onto the table. Under the glaring lights, a nurse places a breathing mask over his bruised and swollen face. The surgeons step forward and begin the operation.

★

Nick leans against a torn fence, scowling and watching André's gang mess around on the run-down playground littered with trash. André saunters over, leans in with a smirk: "Whatcha thinking about? How you gonna find yourself a nice White man when you grow up?"

In a sudden motion, Nick shoves him away and erupts with rage: "Get away from me! *Get the fuck away from me!*"

André stares in surprise.

Nick trembles, on edge, ready to fight come what may.

André gestures for him to calm down: "Hey, take it easy, rough rider. I know before, when you spoke outta line, I gave it to you bad. But you my boy, boy. It's cool."

"It's not cool! What we did... This ain't right. This is– this is fucked up!"

The entire gang stares in alarm.

"Chill, brother," André says. "We gotta fight for our people."

"You ain't my brother. You ain't my people. My people are better than this." Nick swallows hard. "I'm done. I'm fucking done with this shit." He looks to the other members of the gang. Implores them: "This ain't us."

The gang is shaken.

Zero hesitantly steps forward, glancing between Nick and André. André gives him a deathly glare. Looks around at the rest of the boys. A brief stand-off as André's will crushes all potential defiance; the boys shrink away.

Nick waits a long moment, his eyes darting over their stunned faces. Then abruptly turns and tramps off.

André stares after him in bewilderment, then calls out: "Run away, *Nicky*."

Nick doesn't take the bait and keeps walking, neither speeding up nor slowing down.

André tenses in exasperation. "Don't show your faggot face here again!"

Nick keeps walking, without looking back.

André notices Clam Face staring at him and snaps: "What?! What the fuck you looking at?"

Outside KYLX, a reporter interviews a young Black hipster in the crowd. "If Reggie Miles was a White man, the cops would never let this drag on. They'd help him. They'd get him out," the hipster says. "Instead, they're letting him be a prisoner on his own show!"

Forty yards away, another reporter interviews a middle-aged White housewife. "What he's saying – I mean, all these issues… Why is this coming from some guy with a gun? Why isn't it on TV? Why doesn't the media talk about this stuff?" She looks the reporter in the eyes: "Why don't *you* talk about it?"

★

"...Our fathers struggled and bled to build this country," says Tom, "and we're just pissing it away."

"Tom, we need to make progress," says Jake. "What are your demands?"

"You know my demands."

"Yes, truth and respect. But we need to get more specific."

"How much more specific can I get?"

"Help me out here," Jake says. "I'm on your side."

"Jake, who do you work for?"

"I work for you, Tom. I work for the people of this city."

"Does that include your own people?"

"That includes all the people."

"So the people vote on what your orders are?"

"I take my orders from the on-scene commander,"

Jake says.

Hearing this, Ray tenses and grinds his teeth.

"And your commander takes his orders from above," Tom says, "all the way up the food chain: the police chief, the mayor, the governor, the man in Washington."

"Okay, so I'm just a government stooge trying to serve and protect."

"How can you serve or protect your own people when you work for the government that's waging war on us?"

"Where do you think you are – Nazi Germany? Communist Russia?"

"Getting there," Tom says.

"It's still a democracy. Government by the people and for the people, remember?"

"You kidding? We haven't had a government by the people in decades."

"Then what do we have?" Jake asks.

"A government by bankers, lawyers, and corporations."

"Look, I know the government isn't perfect–"

"Not perfect?" Tom breaks in. "It's a goddamn monster sucking the life from us. Killing our jobs. Wrecking our communities."

"C'mon."

"This is– this is your country! Your *home*. They're turning your home into a Third World hellhole."

"You're still free to speak your truth and demand your respect."

"Free? We're not free. The government wipes its bloated ass with our Constitution."

"Tom–"

"Invading our privacy. Meddling in our lives. Telling us what to teach our kids."

"The government's not your enemy, Tom."

"The government wages endless war all over the world but won't protect our own borders!" Tom says. "The government robs us blind. Robs our families, our children. And hands over our wages to criminals and parasites!"

Outside, the crowd seethes.

Jake sighs. "Democracy isn't easy…"

"Democracy?" Tom scoffs. "The Founding Fathers are rolling in their graves." His eyes roam the booth, and he calls out: "Can you hear me? We trusted you. Voted for you. And you sold us out."

Ray looks daggers at Jake, who frowns as he thinks. "So what do you want me to do, Tom?" Jake finally says.

"You want demands?" Tom says. "Here are my demands. Seal the border. Ban racial preferences. And get the damn government out of our lives. That enough for you?"

"I'll see what I can do." Jake clicks off his earpiece. Stares into space.

Ray jolts him out of his thoughts: "What do you think this is, some kind of experiment? A science fair project? I told you— I told you, the brass will have our balls for this!"

"Ray… Captain, sir, I'm just doing my job."

"It's not your job to debate racial… philosophy or whatever he's yammering about."

"It's my job to establish trust."

"You're not here to be his buddy," Ray says. "You're here to negotiate terms of fucking surrender."

"Trust takes time."

"Instead of worrying why he's spouting all this shit, why don't you man up and let him know who's in charge!"

Jake watches Ray intently for a long moment. "What are you so afraid of?"

Ray scowls. "You're dancing in a goddamn minefield here."

"Is this… coming from above?"

"Kid… you have no idea the people you're messing with."

"That's right, sir, I don't," Jake says. "Who are they?"

Ray leans in, his gaze fixed and intense: "Keep pushing, and you'll be lucky to find work as a meter maid."

Taken aback, Jake gapes at him, at a loss for words.

Ray regains his composure. "You have ninety minutes, Lieutenant. Then we cut transmission."

★

Silent and serious, the surgeons labor to suck out the blood clots and repair the ruptured arteries in Billy's brain.

★

In the dusty basement, Colton places a tablet on the pool table. Its screen shows a city map. He points to a patch of green: "Here?"

"Yeah," says Smiley. "A few blocks from the school."

"You sure?"

"It's their hangout. At least that's what Derek says."

"And you're sure it's them?"

"He heard them talking. They... they were bragging about it."

Colton tenses, hands clenching into fists. "If we're lucky, we'll take 'em by surprise."

The boys, circled around the tablet, take in his words, looking apprehensive. Travis reluctantly speaks up:

"Colt… maybe we should just, you know, call the cops?"

"It's a Black-on-White crime. You think those bastards will get what they deserve?"

The gang is silent.

Colton's face hardens: "White boys aren't on the protected list. You won't even see it on the news."

"Why?" asks Smiley.

"The races are all wrong. Doesn't fit their agenda."

Smiley blinks.

Travis looks down, swallows hard.

Colton looks over his friends' grave faces. "It's alright. I'm scared too." He turns to the Confederate battle flag on the wall: "That's why we have this flag."

He comes up to it. Slides his fingers along its fabric. "Why do we have this?" he asks his gang.

They gape at him and the flag, not knowing how to react.

"'Cause this flag means we're free men," Colton says. "It means the system doesn't own us. Doesn't tell us how to live. What to believe. What to hate or what to love. This flag is our honor."

The boys take it in.

"And if we let evil against our people go unpunished, if we're too scared to stand up for our own, then we're not worthy of this flag. And that's a hell of a lot worse than anything the Blacks or Mestizos or anyone else can dish out."

The gang is moved.

Smiley steps forward, taking a deep breath: "Let's do it."

Travis joins him: "Yeah."

Sam nods.

Otto rolls his shoulders and juts out his chin.

"Are we… bringing the guns?" Smiley asks.

"We come packing," Colton says, "but we don't draw till they do."

"Honor," says Sam.

Colton nods grimly.

Smiley frowns. "Are we gonna…"

"No. Not all of them," Colton says. "But their leader gets it."

The cops look on edge as they struggle to control the ever-growing crowd and keep the White, Black, and Mestizo throngs apart. Someone in the Mestizo throng kicks down a barricade. Her eyes darting across the unruly crowd, Linda reaches for her walkie-talkie: "Captain, we're stretched thin out here, and we have a mob of angry... we have an influx of Hispanics and African Americans in the crowd, sir."

In the command center, Ray grimaces. "Get me riot control."

"Tom, we need to– we need to end this," says Jake, his controlled calm fraying under Ray's impatient stare. "You said what you had to–"

"You're still not thinking!" Tom interrupts. "When are you gonna think?"

"Think about what?"

"About your future," Tom says. "The future you're creating for your sons. And for their sons."

"My sons – and my future grandchildren – will be just fine."

"Your grandchildren will be a powerless minority in a giant ghetto."

"They may be a minority, but they won't be powerless. They can hold their own with everyone else."

"You still think all the people of the world are gonna hold hands and sing 'Kumbaya?'"

"Maybe. Someday."

"The other tribes, other races, they don't have our moral dilemmas, our misplaced guilt," Tom says. "When there's enough of them, they'll simply vote themselves more and more of what's ours. Just like they did to the Whites in Bolivia. And Haiti. And Ecuador. Just like they're already doing in California and New York."

"I… appreciate your concern for my future grandchildren."

"They'll punish them just for being White."

Jake shakes his head. "This country's big enough for all of us. The American dream's big enough for all of us."

"Your grandkids won't even know what that means. Their world will be poor, crowded, and dirty."

"So now it's about the environment?" Jake smirks. "You think diversity's to blame for global warming?"

"What do you think the brown baby boom will do to our natural world?" Tom asks.

"What are you talking about?"

"All those new consumers. Tens, hundreds of millions. What's their carbon footprint? How many trees cut down? How many tons of trash?"

"We'll find a solution. If not in my sons' generation, then the next."

"Wishful thinking. Your grandkids will live in tyranny."

"My grandkids will learn their history, and they won't give up their liberty."

"You think government schools will teach them real history? Real science? Real liberty?"

"I sure hope so," Jake sighs.

"You think political correctness is bad now," Tom says, "wait another ten years. The minorities will vote us a brand new Communism."

"You can see the future?"

"They've been laying the groundwork for a century. Centralizing power. Weakening borders. Growing the government like a pig on steroids. You think they're gonna stop?"

"Who is this 'they' out to get White people?" Jake asks.

"The ones running this circus, they don't care if you're White or Black or purple. Who you pray to, or what flag you wave. They don't give a damn if Americans lose their jobs. If Muslims take over Europe and kill Jews and Christians," Tom says. "They hate borders. And they love 'diversity.'"

Reggie looks up at him, surprised at his words.

"Who are these people?" Jake asks. "What do they want?"

"There's nothing they'd love more than to breed us

all together. Breed us all down into the same generic mongrel. With no race, no history, no real culture," Tom says. "The perfect wage slave. The ideal consumer. Because he's a product himself."

Outside, the crowd of all races absorbs his words, growing strangely quiet.

"Why would anyone want a world like that?" Jake asks.

"The people pulling the strings, their only concern, their only loyalty, their only faith – is their bottom line," Tom says.

Jake frowns, blinks. "You think race mixing will bring down civilization?"

"This is… our genetic essence. What we are as a people," Tom says. "We lose that, we're done for."

Ray grabs his walkie-talkie: "Mikey, cut the AC."

Taken aback, Jake turns, and the two men lock eyes.

"If the bastard wants to keep yammering," Ray says, "he can do it in a fucking sauna."

★

Riot cops arrive at the radio station, wearing armor and carrying shields and batons, their helmets glistening in the scorching sun. They take positions along the barricades. The crowd pulls back, thwarted… for now.

★

"…Our civilization is crumbling," says Tom. "All over the world, we're losing our land. All over the world, our numbers are falling."

"So what do you want me to do about it?" Jake asks, frowning at his watch.

"Not sinking in, is it?" Tom says. "Your race is dying. *Your people* are dying!"

Reggie shakes his head.

"What do you want to do," Jake asks, "pay White people to have babies?"

"Better that than what our elites are doing."

"Which is?"

"Replacing us with people from the Third World."

"Well, if we're dying out... someone has to replace us, right?"

"Do you think you can have a First World nation with Third World people?" asks Tom.

Jake hesitates. "I hope so."

"Do you honestly believe people can change what they are just by moving to a different country?"

Jake tenses, gulps. "I suppose not."

"So what do you think's gonna happen to our country?"

"I don't know," Jake says, his mouth dry.

"Yeah, you do," Tom says. "And someday, when your grandchildren sit in your lap and ask you why their country is one giant ghetto, you're gonna have to look them in the eyes and tell them it's because you buried your head in the sand. Because you didn't stand up for your people. Because you didn't fight for truth and respect."

A flock of TV news helicopters circles over the KYLX radio station, their cameras shooting the cops and the crowd and transmitting the footage to live broadcasts all around the country.

A spring rider in the shape of a pony sticks out of the dead grass, its spring rusted, its paint peeling. Atop it sits a beat-up boombox. From its speakers rumbles Tom's voice: "...How long are we gonna deny it? How long will we cover it up? The crimes against our people. Blacks, Mestizos, we know what you do to us..."

André listens, frowning, as his gang fools around on the playground, trying to stay in the shade.

"Hell, I know it's ugly," Tom says. "But that doesn't mean we get to look away."

Clam Face waddles over: "Yo, André, you wanna see the–"

"Shhhh." André flips off the radio. Turns toward the fence.

Silence and stillness… Then Tiago's gang slowly emerges out of the shadows, keeping close.

André's boys rise and converge. A tense moment as the two gangs size each other up. Then Tiago steps forward: "What up, André?"

"Not much… ese," André says.

Tiago cautiously approaches, glances at the boombox: "You been listening to the radio?"

André nods and steps forward, narrowing his eyes in the bright sun.

The two meet halfway, their gangs standing at the ready.

"You see how we got a problem together?" asks Tiago.

After a moment, André nods.

"You wanna double up our numbers?" Tiago asks.

"Why? You see something coming?"

"I see gabachos trying to take back the streets."

"Yeah – *trying*," André sneers. The two boys chuckle,

the tension easing up all around. Tiago sticks out his fist. After a moment of hesitation, André bumps knuckles with him.

★

The Firebird races down the freeway. Colton drives, icy resolve in his eyes, as the radio plays on: "…Why are we letting this happen? Why are we letting them do this to us?!" asks Tom. "This is *our* country!"

Smiley, riding shotgun, fidgets in his seat and rubs his neck. Behind him, Sam and Travis glance at each other, jittery with adrenaline. Next to them, Otto breathes heavily, his shoulders tight, a deep frown on his face. Abruptly he leans toward Colton: "Hey, man, this is some real… heavy shit. You sure you wanna do this?"

"If we don't, who will?" says Colton.

★

Feeling frazzled, Jake grabs a water bottle from the cooler and exits the command center. He comes up to a window, gulps down the cold liquid, and wipes his mouth, staring out at the roiling mob at the barricades.

"You know, this used to be Mexico." Hector's voice startles Jake.

"Used to be," Jake agrees.

Hector approaches and looks out the window. "You're on the air. Everybody can hear. Why didn't you... why didn't you say something?"

Jake turns to face him: "About what?"

"You think that too, Jake – that we're all parasites with no honor?" Hector's hands clench into fists.

"Hector, this is no time for–"

"You think I should bow down and kiss your feet 'cause you let me live here?"

"I think maybe Mayland's right, and no one trusts each other."

"I work. I pay my taxes. I speak English as good as

anyone. And I don't hide any illegals in my basement."

"Please don't make this day any harder."

"I fought in this country's stupid war."

"Hector–"

"I know this comes as a big shock to you, amigo, but you don't have to be White to be a real American."

At the barricades, a hooded Black youth glowers at a hard-edged White youth several yards away. "You got a problem?" the White youth asks.

"Fuck you, cracker."

Scowling, the White youth steps forward, joined by his friends and other White onlookers. The Black youth, his homies, and other Black bystanders start toward the White group, eager for a fight.

The riot cops rush in between the two groups, separating the Whites and the Blacks.

★

With the AC cut off, the broadcast booth is turning into an oven. Tom and Reggie glare at each other, tense, their faces wet with sweat.

"…What, you don't wanna talk about slavery?" says Reggie. "You don't have any facts or stats or clever words about the millions of African people stuffed like cargo into slave ships? Starved. Beaten. Degraded. Dying from disease. From hunger. From the White man's lash."

Outside, a current of tension passes through the Black throng.

"The slaves have been dead for centuries," says Tom. "And so have the slave owners."

"These are my people, my ancestors!" Reggie says.

"You were never a slave. Neither was your dad, or his dad, or his dad's dad. White people haven't oppressed you – they gave you your own show!"

"Oppression takes many forms."

"You don't even know what oppression means."

"You don't know nothing about me!"

"I know you don't get to blame ancient atrocities for your problems."

"So we should just be good Negros and smile and get on with it?"

"That's right," Tom says. "Unless your victim badge is all you've got."

"We should just forget the two and a half centuries of exploitation. How our ancestors were branded like livestock. Whipped. Raped. Castrated. Is that what you want us to forget?"

"I'm not asking you to forget," Tom says. "Just remember that we're not the same White people. Only one in thirteen families ever had slaves. And most immigrants came after the slaves were freed."

"That's funny. No one's responsible. And yet, here we are."

"Who do you think sold the slaves to the slave traders?"

"What the hell you talking about?"

"I'm talking about all those Black people – African kings, warlords, kidnappers – who sold *twelve million* of their own people into slavery. Sold them for White man's gold.

"Who says they sold them?"

"Records do," Tom says. "Or how about all those Black slave owners in the South? No one ever talks about them."

Reggie looks aside, grinding his teeth. "This country was built on our backs. With our sweat. Our blood. Our tears. This country – this country owes us!"

Outside, people in the Black throng nod as they listen.

"You owe us a debt," says Reggie. "Where are our reparations?"

"You *got* your reparations," says Tom. "Trillions in welfare. Food, education, housing, jobs."

"Not enough."

"Integration. Race quotas. A Presidential apology."

"Not enough."

"Trillions for all the cops, the lawyers, the prisons – to hold all your thieves, your rapists, your murderers," says Tom. "Not to mention the Civil War and the six hundred thousand dead White soldiers."

"You owe us *real* reparations!" says Reggie. "The Jews got theirs. The Japs got theirs. You owe–"

"You want more?! You want more?!" Tom snaps, pointing his gun at Reggie. "Where are our reparations for the *tens of millions* of burglaries, muggings, assaults?! For all the White women raped by Blacks! For over *sixty thousand* murders!"

Tom's voice crackles from the boombox and fills the playground: "...Blacks have murdered more White Americans than died in Vietnam!"

On edge, André changes the station. Gangster rap blares from the speakers. He sprawls on the ruined merry-go-round. Takes a deep breath. Looks from Tiago's gang to his own. "Zero," he calls out, "gimme that blunt."

"I only got one left," the skinny boy says.

André stares him down. Reluctantly, Zero hands over the marijuana cigar.

André lights it. Inhales deeply. Exhales a big cloud of smoke, relaxing.

Nearby, Clam Face shakes a spray can and paints an illegible mess of letters on the spiral slide.

"What the fuck is that?" André asks.

"Our new tag," the fat boy says.

André glances at Tiago, who smirks at him and looks away. Tensing again, André gets up and steps toward Clam Face: "That ain't no tag. It's what your mama's cunt looks like. Gimme that." He yanks the can out of Clam Face's hand. Clam Face opens his mouth but says nothing.

★

Under the searing sun, the Whites and the Blacks outside KYLX have gathered into opposing camps, each brimming with indignation.

★

In the broadcast booth, Tom and Reggie are soaked with sweat, their nerves strained to the limit.

"…It's like you said, Tom – everyone else's having a baby boom while your people are dying," says Reggie.

"Most of the army is still White," says Tom.

"How many gang members out there? They all got guns."

"You think you can take us?"

"Your old White world's running out of time. Better be real nice."

Tom's eyes narrow. "Are you threatening me? Are you threatening my people?"

Reggie spreads his hands: "Just pointing out the inevitable."

"Nothing's inevitable," Tom says. "We've been kind. We want peace. But if your race threatens my race, we will wipe you out."

"Soon you'll be less than half this country."

Tom sneers. "If we're a tenth of this country, we can

still kill the lot of you before supper."

Reggie absorbs this, his expression darkening. A bitter smirk spreads across his lips. "You say you want truth and respect. You come here screaming your facts and numbers. But it's all just a fancy mask for your hate."

Tom stiffens.

"You want truth?" Reggie says. "How about the truth in your heart?"

"Is that your way of calling me racist?"

"C'mon! You don't need to call me nigger to let me know how you feel. What's the truth in here?!" Reggie thumps his chest with his fist. "You hate us. *You hate my people.*"

For a long moment, Tom just stares at him. Then he says, "I hate your damn horde of thieves and rapists and murderers. I hate your stupid ghetto culture that celebrates pimps and drug dealers. I hate how you won't take responsibility for your own streets. For your own children."

Outside, the Black throng listens, agape.

"I hate how you still think we owe you something," Tom says.

Reggie nods, glaring, his jaw set.

"But I don't hate your people," Tom sighs. "Hell, every people must find their way. But not like this. Not on the back of another people."

"We're not on your fucking back!"

The two lock eyes.

"Is this what you want?" Tom asks. "Is this what you want for your people? Chasing like dogs after government scraps. Corrupt politicians treating you like stupid children. Women without husbands. Children without fathers. Men living and dying in prisons."

Outside, the Black throng listens, frozen.

"Growing weaker and weaker. More and more dependent on the government," Tom says. "This is a whole new kind of slavery."

Reggie swallows hard, his eyes glistening. "Damn… *Damn*… We followed the wrong brother. Should've listened to Brother Malcolm. Should have walked away. Fearless. Proud." He looks up at Tom. "Then I wouldn't have to deal with the likes of you."

"I'm the best friend you've got. If this is not just for show," Tom says. "Do you love your people?

"Yeah, I love my people."

"I want your people to be strong and good and free."

Reggie is taken aback.

In the command center, Jake listens in, equally surprised.

"Be brave," Tom says. "Take responsibility. Create something. For yourselves. For your neighborhoods. For your race."

Outside, the Black throng takes in his words, quiet and still.

"Love your people," Tom says. "And let us love ours."

The Firebird cruises down a city street. Behind the wheel, Colton scans the grimy milieu with the eyes of a hunter:

Trash on the asphalt. Boarded-up buildings. Graffiti. Homeless people. More trash.

In the passenger seat, Smiley takes deep breaths, trying hard to be brave. He looks at the GPS on his phone. "We're getting close," he says, his voice strained.

In the back, Travis and Sam silently psych each other up.

Next to them, Otto breathes fast and hard, his face drenched with sweat. Suddenly he pleads, "Colt, pull over."

The Firebird pulls over to the curb, and Otto hurries out of the car.

Travis leans toward Sam: "I think big boy needs to change his diapers."

Otto staggers over to a graffitied storefront and vomits violently. He straightens. Wipes his mouth. Paces in the dirt, breathing heavily, as the Firebird's idling engine quietly rumbles. Finally, he comes up to Colton's window.

Colton gazes straight ahead.

"I think I ate something rotten or something," Otto says.

Colton keeps his gaze forward, refusing to look at him.

"Hey, man, maybe... what if... there could be a lot more of them than us." Otto frowns, his face pale. "They're niggers – who knows what kind of guns they got."

"You with us, or are you just talk?"

"I know I said I... but this is... this is... I can't do this. You understand. You get it. Right?"

Colton steps on the gas, and the Firebird roars ahead, leaving Otto staring after it in a cloud of dust.

"...We're a different race – a separate people," Tom says, fighting thirst and fatigue. "We have the right to our own neighborhoods. Our own culture. Our own way of life!"

"Some people would call you a racist for saying that," says Jake.

"I don't care what they call me. 'Racist' is just a scary word they use to keep us from thinking."

"White supremacy has been nothing but disaster."

"So has White guilt."

"This country has trouble enough–"

"This country was founded by White pioneers. Paid for with White lives. Built on White faith, White laws, White science. We're the brain, the backbone, and the beating heart of this country!"

Outside, the White throng absorbs Tom's words, chins high, eyes agleam.

"Why shouldn't we be supreme here?" Tom says. "Or at least left the fuck alone!"

A chant starts and spreads through the White throng, building in intensity: "Mayland! Mayland! Mayland!"

The Blacks and the Mestizos glare at the Whites, the two groups united by fear and fury.

The riot cops stand at the ready, shield to shield.

★

Jake scarfs down an energy bar and stares into space, thinking.

"It's over, Jake." Ray's voice jerks him out of his thoughts.

Jake looks at his watch. "I still have twenty-three minutes."

"Man, you're some piece of work." Ray shakes his head. "I thought you were good."

"I *am* good, sir. I'm good because I don't cut corners."

Ray smirks. "I thought every man has his levers?"

"Some levers are best left alone."

"I'm not sure who's pulling whose levers here."

"I'm in control of the situation, sir," Jake says. "Please let me–"

Ray's cell phone rings, interrupting him. Ray answers. "Yeah... When?... And you're telling me this *now*?!... I don't care what Levitz said... Fucking Christ." He hangs up, frowning. After a pause, he says, "Someone beat up Mayland's kid."

Jake's eyes widen in alarm.

"He's in a coma. They don't yet know how bad it is."

Jake gulps. "Where is he now?"

"County hospital."

The two take a moment to absorb the news. Getting an idea, Ray looks up: "You gotta tell him. Tell him his son's in the hospital. Tell him Billy needs him."

"That's a bad idea," Jake says. "We'd be risking a murder-suicide."

"All this time, you've been telling me he's not a killer!"

"He isn't. But he is a desperate man. And if you push him over the edge, he might do something stupid."

"We'll have to take our chances."

Still wary of each other, André's and Tiago's respective gangs share the playground and listen to the radio:

"…They don't respect us," says Tom. "Latinos put Latinos first – and to hell with the stupid Anglos who let them in."

"Tom, please," says Jake.

"Latinos hire Latinos. Rent to Latinos. Vote for Latinos. Demand racial privileges. Everything for La Raza. Nothing for us."

Reggie butts in: "What're you complaining about? Mexicans work for your people. It's my people whose jobs they're taking. My people they're pushing from our hoods. My people they're killing in the streets."

On the playground, tension once again fills the air. Members of each gang squint and scowl at those of the other.

"While your kids learn Spanish, our kids fight and die resisting the invasion," Reggie says. "All the gangs are already at war. In the prisons. In the schools."

Clam Face looks down, blinking and frowning.

Luis kicks an empty can on the ground.

"My cousin's kid lost an eye 'cause he said the wrong thing to a cholo," Reggie says.

The gangs tense up more and more. André glares at Tiago, clenches his fists. Tiago trades glances with Mateo and Luis.

"Then why aren't your leaders doing something?" asks Tom.

"I don't know," says Reggie. "But it's about fucking time."

Behind his back, André's fingers slowly reach underneath the merry-go-round... and find the Glock taped to its base. Heartened by the warm metal, André considers his options.

Tiago looks around at André's gang, finding the playground less and less welcoming with every passing moment. Wound-up muscles. Stern faces. Cold eyes.

He steps over to the boombox and turns it off. Then looks up at André. "We should go." Luis and Mateo join him, looking fazed.

"Yeah, you do that," André says, his voice hard.

Tiago motions to his friends, and they march off as André's gang stares after them. Zero hesitates, then offers an uncertain goodbye: "Peace."

Tiago's gang doesn't respond.

Zero turns to André: "Hey– I thought– what's going on?"

"It's a bad deal," André says grimly. "Can't trust 'em."

"What about the crackers?"

"They're worse than the crackers. The crackers got laws and rules. The chili shitters, they'll kill us all when they don't need us no more."

★

Tiago's gang emerges from the alley into the piercing sunlight. Luis falters. "Move your ass, wey," Tiago says.

"I thought we were gonna make alliances?" says Luis.

Tiago scowls. "You can't make alliances with animals."

Down the street, a car appears, traveling toward them... a Pontiac Firebird.

★

Behind the wheel, Colton spots moving figures up ahead. On edge, he and his friends watch as a group of tattooed Mestizo youths draws closer. Smiley clutches the sawed-off shotgun.

"Hold it," says Colton. "It's not them."

"They aren't even Black," says Sam.

"Good eyes there, buddy," says Travis. "You're a real sharpshooter."

"Wh– who are they?" Smiley asks.

"Don't know," says Colton.

"Are they... enemies?"

"Not unless they start something."

Tiago's gang gets into a black SUV. Its engine rumbles to life. The wheels screech as the SUV speeds away.

More and more Mestizos appear at the barricades around KYLX, keeping their distance from both the Whites and the Blacks.

★

"...We've forgotten the Alamo. We've forgotten Goliad," says Tom. "Mexico treats us like a colony. A dumping ground. And we just bend over and take it."

"Tom, we have to end this," says Jake. "Please, be reasonable."

"Reasonable? The Mexican government prints booklets telling illegals how to sneak into our country!"

"They aren't all Mexicans."

"It's the whole Third World!"

"It's a complex situation. They have their reasons for coming here."

"They treat our borders like a joke. Meddle in our government. Flood us with poverty, drugs, and crime."

"Listen–"

"This is an invasion! An act of war."

Outside, the Mestizo throng fumes.

"Jesus," Jake sighs. "Mexico's our ally. Our trading partner. Our next-door neighbor."

"What kind of ally invades our borders? What kind

of partner subverts our economy? What kind of neighbor tries to steal our land?"

"They think... some of them believe... this land was stolen from them," Jake says.

Reggie blinks, cocks his head.

"We signed a treaty," Tom says. "We paid for this land. For empty land on the outskirts – with barely eighty thousand living here!"

Jake looks at the scowling Hector and tenses. "They can hear you, Tom."

For a moment, Tom gazes at the glowing "ON AIR" sign. Fighting fatigue and thirst, his clothes drenched with sweat, he finds his words...

"Mexicans, Muslims, all you people of the world... We built these streets, these cities, these homes. Our churches stand here. Our fathers are buried here. This is White man's land. And you will not take it from us!"

Outside, the White throng listens, gripped by a newfound sense of unity.

Tom paces, gripping his gun and gathering steam. "How'd you like it if tens of millions of White people

161

poured into your country? Marched on your streets. Rioted. Demanded you pay for all our needs. How'd you like it if we demanded racial privileges and took your jobs?"

The White and Mestizo throngs bristle at each other, and the riot cops move in between them.

"Would you celebrate your new 'diversity?'" Tom asks. "Or would you kick us out?"

Hector turns and glowers at Jake.

Tom spreads his hands, searching for words. A moment of vulnerability… "We're not your enemies. We can be friends. We can work together. Trade. Learn from each other. Help each other." He faces Reggie, and their eyes meet. "But please let us live in peace on our own land with our own people!" He turns away, his expression darkening. "Or this will be the first drop of a tsunami."

Reggie gulps.

★

Jake splashes cold water on his face. Looks up in the mirror at his weary reflection.

"Jake."

Hearing Hector's voice, Jake stiffens. Sighing, he turns: "What?"

"I'm sorry."

It takes the surprised Jake a moment to process this and lower his guard.

"You didn't deserve what I said." Hector steps closer.

"It's fine," Jake says. "It's alright."

"I just... I know about the gangs and the crime, but... that's not... it's not who we are. He's making us all into..." Hector frowns.

"He didn't say all, uh, Latinos are..."

"Yeah. I know. Just made me angry, you know."

Jake nods.

"I've been thinking... I resent the fucker. But I get him. He wants to save his people... his raza," Hector says. "Fuck, if I thought my people were in danger...

man, I hope I'd have the guts to pull something like this."

Jake absorbs this, at a loss for words. Then wipes his face with a paper towel.

Hector smirks. "He's so scared for his precious Anglo culture... Tell him, if he surrenders, I'll let him try these sapotes dulces my wife makes. Once he's tasted that, he'll want more Mexicans in this country."

★

More and more helicopters buzz over the radio station and the boiling crowd.

At the barricades, a reporter interviews an angry White man. "Tom Mayland is the last honest man in this country," the man says. "He's got the balls to say what everyone's afraid to say. The man's a fucking hero!"

Fifty yards away, another reporter interviews an equally angry Mestizo man. "What the hell's going on here? Whose side are the cops on? This guy's a racist!"

the man says. "What kind of cops are these?! These are racist cops!"

★

The phone rings relentlessly. Ray stares at it. Finally, he answers. "Chief, I'm–"

"Vallero, you listen good," interrupts the Chief of Police. "My phone's been ringing nonstop. The mayor, the governor, NAACP, NCLR – every minority rights group is on my ass!"

"I just wanted–"

"You know what they're saying on the news? The last thing this department needs is charges of racism!"

"Chief–"

"End it. End this farce. Or your career is done." The Chief slams down the phone.

Ray swallows hard, wide-eyed and pale.

★

Insults fly back and forth at the barricades, and a brawl between the Blacks and the Mestizos is about to break out. The riot cops rush in to separate them.

★

"This negotiation is finished," says Ray. "Tell him to put down the gun and come out with his hands up."

"Please. Ray. Let me end this well," Jake pleads.

"This is it. Last chance, kid."

Jake clicks on his earpiece, dials, and waits as Ray stares him down... Tom answers. "Tom... are you thirsty?" Jake asks.

A long moment as Tom considers his response and Reggie watches him intently, both parched, their faces glistening with sweat.

"I'm fine," Tom says.

"How about you, Mr. Miles?"

"I don't need nothing," Reggie says and coughs.

"Let me bring you some water – just in case," Jake says.

Ray stiffens and bites his lip, glowering.

"You and that SWAT team out there?" Tom asks.

"Just me."

"More tricks up your sleeve?"

"No tricks – just a bottle of cold H_2O."

Tom looks at Reggie. Wavers... "Alright."

Jake hangs up. "What the fuck are you doing?" Ray demands.

"Taking my last chance."

Clutching a bottle of Aquafina, Jake steps down the corridor past the SWAT team, who look at him askance. Taking deep breaths, he cautiously approaches the broadcast booth. Knocks. Very slowly and carefully, he opens the door. "Tom, it's me. I'm unarmed." He peeks in...

The air is thick with sweat and anger. Tense, Tom holds his gun aimed at Reggie, who looks understandably anxious. "If you try something, I *will* shoot him," Tom says.

"Understood." Jake offers him the bottle.

"Drugged?"

Jake opens it and takes a sip.

Tom motions toward the console: "Put it there. Slowly."

Careful not to make any sudden movements, Jake steps over to the console and sets down the bottle. Turning, he takes a step toward Tom.

"That's far enough."

Jake looks him in the eyes. "Tom... I can't keep this going. Please. You don't want to jeopardize your life for this."

Tom swallows hard. "What is one man's life next to the fate of our race?"

The broadcast booth door slowly opens...

The SWAT team aim their rifles, ready for any

surprises.

Jake emerges and trudges past the cops, seemingly unaware of them.

Tom guzzles the water. Noticing Reggie staring, he stops and offers him the half-full bottle. Reggie wavers, reluctant to accept it, but thirst gets the better of him – he takes the bottle and drinks.

Heavyhearted, Jake enters the command center. Ray looks up at him with a question in his eyes.

Jake sighs and shakes his head.

Doing her best to sound calm and authoritative, Linda bullhorns the simmering crowd: "Remain calm. Anyone who engages in violent or threatening behavior *will* be arrested and prosecu–"

A bottle hurls toward her. Barely missing her head, it crashes into the asphalt and shatters, showering her with glass shards.

The riot cops rush forward, shielding her. She gulps, her heart racing.

As the news spreads all across the country, more and more people turn on their radios and tune into KYLX online.

Eyes ablaze, Tom rants on the air with utmost sincerity:

"...What happened to us? We were brave, strong, proud. The mightiest tribe in all the world. We drove back the Moors, the Mongols, the Muslim hordes. We built the greatest civilization ever – the jewel of history.

Our empires stretched across continents, across oceans…"

Outside, the White throng listens, transfixed.

Tom's expression darkens. "All gone."

★

Jake stares at the phone, frowning and biting his nails.

"Did you tell him?" Ray asks. "About his kid."

"No."

Ray shakes his head. "Doesn't matter. We're cutting transmission." He brings the walkie-talkie to his ear.

"Wait," Jake implores. "Ray… don't do this. Let him say his piece. I can end it – I can talk him down. Just give me a little more time."

"It's not mine to give."

"You're the on-scene commander. It's your call."

"The call's come down from above."

A pause as Jake makes a decision. "You think the Chief will take the blame when this explodes in your face?"

171

The other cops in the room turn to look at the two. Taken aback, Ray lowers the walkie-talkie and gapes at Jake.

"We're losing everything," says Tom. "Our land. Our culture. Our freedom. Everything we are as a people. Our house is burning, and we're pouring gas on the fire. Welcoming our own oblivion."

A tense stillness settles over the White throng.

"Can't you see? This is madness. A disease. A slow suicide. Why are we doing this? Why are we letting them do this to us?!"

"Don't do it," Jake says. "Don't push him over the edge."

Ray's face reddens. "We're not the suicide hotline. We're not a fucking talk show. We're cops. And we'll handle this like cops."

Around the room, the other cops stare in bewilderment.

"Right or wrong, he's just talking," Jake says. "Just talking."

"He's pushing too many buttons," Ray says. "And so are you."

"Isn't that the whole point of the First Amendment – so we can talk it out instead of killing each other?"

Ray sneers. "Get off your high fucking horse, kid."

"This is a good man. A good man doing something stupid and desperate. Help me save them both."

Ray's sneer fades. He shifts uncomfortably. "He's got a hostage. He's making political demands. He's a racist, a terrorist, pure and simple."

Jake stares him down. "Are you so scared of the Chief, you'll risk the lives of two men?"

★

"We forgot... We've forgotten who we are. And we must remember," says Tom. "We are the children of

Shakespeare and Newton and Da Vinci. Kin of Einstein. Pushkin. Nietzsche. Blood of Napoleon. Edison. Washington."

A sense of shared pride kindles and spreads through the White throng.

"All across the world, we're one people. One sacred tribe. The great White race."

"You wanna smear the department, Lieutenant?" asks Ray.

"I want to finish what I started, sir," Jake says.

"He's got inside your head. You're compromised."

"You think internal affairs will believe that?"

Ray stares at him. "You threatening me?"

"I'm trying to save you from disaster."

"We are a great people. And a good people," Tom says. "We have brought science and reason to the darkest corners of the globe. We've stopped wars. Fed and cured millions. Fought for human rights all over the world."

The White throng swells with newfound pride.

Tom looks at Reggie. "For more than half a century, we've treated the other races with incredible kindness. We welcomed them into our society. Gave them all our rights. Spent trillions on them," Tom says. "And if they still think we owe them something, they can go to hell."

"Fuck you and your self-righteous bullshit!" Ray glances around the command center for support. "You think I'm gonna let the whole department burn 'cause of you?!"

"It's not the department you're worried about," Jake says.

Ray steps into Jake's personal space: "Listen, you pompous chatterbox, you think you're better than me?! I'm a real cop. Real cops aren't afraid to get their hands dirty."

"It's not your hands that's dirty."

"You think you can talk me down? I'll have you in handcuffs for obstruction before another arrogant fart leaves your mouth."

Jake offers his upturned wrists: "Go ahead, sir. I'll be in handcuffs for minutes, and you'll be in prison for years."

The other cops watch in alarm.

Ray twitches. Steps toward Jake, seething. Jake holds his ground. A silent stand-off… Ray gulps.

"Our civilization… our race… it's precious and fragile," Tom says. "We're supposed to love each other. Help each other. Protect each other. Our culture. Our neighborhoods. Our women and children."

The White throng, silent and still, absorbs Tom's words.

"Or we will lose it all."

★

Jake reluctantly enters the empty office, and Ray shuts the door behind him. Ray opens his mouth to speak just as his cell phone rings. He looks at it and grits his teeth. Then looks up at Jake. "Jake… kid… think about it. It's over. Why make all this trouble for yourself? In a month or two, no one's gonna remember this."

"I'll remember," says Jake.

"With your brains, you can have *my* job in a few years. You learn the game, you might end up with the Chief's job," Ray says. "This is a golden ticket you got here, kid. Don't piss it away."

Jake frowns. "We're supposed to protect people…"

"We do protect people. But we also protect each other," Ray says. "Don't be naive, Jake. Sometimes you gotta cut a corner or two to get the job done."

"I can't do this," Jake says. "It's against everything my badge stands for."

"Take a good look at that badge of yours."

Hesitantly, Jake takes out his badge.

"Milton PD," Ray says. "Right there on the badge." His phone rings again. He grimaces at it, then peers into Jake's eyes. "What do you say, Jake? Do we understand each other?"

For a long moment, Jake gazes at his badge, frowning... Then he tosses it at Ray's feet and strides out of the room without looking back.

★

"We must wake up. *Wake up.* All of us," Tom says. "Men and women. Young and old. Rich and poor. Straight and gay. This is– this is beyond gender, age, or status. Democrats. Republicans. This is beyond politics. Christians. Jews. Atheists. This is beyond religion. This is... this is our sons and daughters. Our moms and dads. Our siblings, cousins, husbands, wives..." Remembering his own beloved wife, he pauses and swallows hard.

Outside, the White throng waits in rapt attention.

★

Under the blistering sun, Jake wades through the sea of bodies. Breathing in the sweat and anger. Drowning. Tom's voice surges from the radios all around him: "…This is our grandparents, our friends, our neighbors…" He presses forward through the ever-growing crowd, getting farther and farther from the radio station.

"Can't you see…" Tom asks, "can't you see what's at stake here? This is *our people. Our race.*"

Jake stops. Gulps. Looks back, wavering… Then he faces forward and disappears into the crowd.

★

Ray leans on the desk and listens to the broadcast, a strange melancholy in his eyes.

"Paris, London, New York, LA – how many cities must burn before we wake up? How many daughters must be raped? How many sons murdered?" Tom asks. "What are we afraid of? Traitors? Strangers who call us names?"

The walkie-talkie weighs heavy in Ray's hand as he slowly raises it to his ear. "Mikey, cut the power."

★

"Brothers, sisters… we need to stand up for ourselves. Proud and brave, like our fathers were. *We must unite.* Or America will be a Third World ghetto and Europe a Muslim prison," Tom says, his face slick with sweat. "We must stand as one. Or all is lost–"

The lights on the booth's walls and ceiling dim with a low thrum, plunging Tom into darkness. He looks around, alarmed.

Amidst the black, the phone light flickers red.

Reggie looks up at Tom, who hesitates, then picks up the phone.

"This is Captain Ray Vallero. We have some bad news. Your son... had an accident. We need you to come out and help us to–"

Tom breaks in, dazed by Ray's words: "Is this... what kind of... what are you..."

"Billy needs you right now."

"He's... he is... wh– where is he? Where is my son?!"

"I'm telling you, he was injured–"

"What have you done to him?"

"I didn't do any–"

"Where is he?! Put him on the phone. Get Billy on the phone right now, or I'll shoot him!" He points the gun at Reggie.

Reggie tenses, eyes darting between Tom and the gun.

"Listen to me–" Ray begins.

"Let me talk to my son!" Tom demands. "Let me talk to him, or I'll–"

He drops the phone as Reggie tackles him. The two crash onto the floor. Muscles clenched, faces locked in a grimace, they wrestle for the gun.

★

In the driver's seat of his Firebird, Colton peers through binoculars, the glass glinting in the harsh sun. Frowning, he watches André's gang on the abandoned playground.

Sam quietly prays. Travis glowers out the window, grinding his teeth. Smiley takes deep breaths, clinging to the shotgun.

Colton lowers the binoculars and looks over the faces of his gang. The boys share a moment, united in vengeful purpose. Tension builds.

Setting his jaw, Colton nods.

They emerge from the car and march toward the playground, aflame with adrenaline.

Colton kicks down the rusted chain-link gate. It flies off the hinges and clatters toward André's gang.

André and his boys turn in alarm.

Clam Face freezes, mouth agape.

Zero stumbles back: "Oh, shit!"

André scrambles to the merry-go-round and drops

down, reaching under the base. He rips his Glock off its bottom and raises it, aiming at Smiley.

Now it's Smiley who freezes, eyes wide, the shotgun dead metal in his hands.

Colton instantly whips out his .44 Magnum and fires.

André's gun hand bursts into bloody chunks. His Glock clanks along the ground. Turning pale, André stares in shock at his mangled arm.

Colton puts away the .44 as he nears the closest member of André's gang. He grabs Clam Face's head and elbows him in the face, sending blood and teeth flying.

Colton's gang plows into André's gang. A brutal melee erupts.

★

The phone lies on the floor of the broadcast booth as Tom and Reggie grapple for the gun. Ray's voice crackles out of the receiver: "What's going on in there?!"

A loud boom echoes in the booth as the gun goes off.

Reggie punches Tom in the face. Then again. Bloodied and riled, Tom twists and elbows Reggie in the temple. Reggie's grasp loosens, and Tom yanks the gun free and swipes him hard with its butt.

Clutching his gun and keeping it trained on Reggie, Tom struggles to his feet. Reggie scrambles back in alarm. The two men glare at each other, wide-eyed, breathing hard, their faces dripping with sweat and blood. The gun aimed at Reggie's chest trembles in Tom's hand. A long, tense moment of truth.

Slowly, Tom lowers the gun. Stumbles backward. Slumps against the wall, motionless. Silence...

"I hope my daughter doesn't know," Reggie says finally.

"My son knows..." Tom says.

"How old is he?"

"Seventeen."

"My daughter's seven," Reggie says. "Just started second grade. They're learning about birds, and she can't stop talking about bluejays and robins and woodpeckers..."

"Taisha?"

Reggie nods. "Bill?"

"Billy..." Tom says. "I remember when Billy was seven... Kathy and I took him to the beach, and he's splashing in the waves. We were afraid the ocean would carry him away. He's so small..."

"They ain't small for long."

"No..." Tom agrees. "I wish I could... go back. To my Kathy and Billy... to our home... to our country. Like it was. Like it used to be. Beautiful..."

"You know... it's funny how we don't really see each other," Reggie says. "All we get is... glimpses."

"I see enough."

"You got what you came for," Reggie says. "Go home. Go home, White man."

"It's not over... till I get truth and respect."

"You know, Tom, you are one stubborn motherfucker."

"Look who's talking."

The two look at each other. And they can't help it. They smirk. Smile. Chuckle. The chuckle builds into mutual and unrestrained laughter, all the pent-up tension bursting free. Finally, peace.

Crash! The SWAT team bursts in, assault rifles aimed.

Tom turns, reflexively raising his gun.

Reggie's eyes go wide.

The cops open fire.

Crimson craters erupt in Tom's chest as he jerks back from the impact.

"No!!!" Reggie screams.

Tom gazes at the cops, tottering, a strange calm in his eyes. And then he crumples to the floor.

Reggie clambers to his feet. Pushes past the cops. Gapes in shock at Tom's shattered corpse, splayed out in a spreading pool of blood.

The vast crowd is silent. Faces of all races stare at the radio station in alarm and confusion. As the White, Black, and Mestizo throngs reach different understandings of what just happened, murmurs of outrage course through the crowd, building to a critical mass. The three mobs glare at each other and the cops, eyes narrowing, muscles tensing, fingers curling into fists.

★

Hector checks Tom's pulse and shakes his head. Ray steps toward the stunned Reggie.

A cop with a flurried face and a phone in his hand gets between them: "Captain, we're getting calls from all over the city."

Ray's walkie-talkie crackles to life, and he gestures for the cop to wait.

★

"The crowd's out of control," Linda shouts into her walkie-talkie over the clamor of the three mobs. "It's about to get real ugly out here."

Hooting and howling, the frantic crowd surrounds the riot cops, who are trapped between the three mobs with nowhere to go. The cops raise their shields and hold their ground as the rioters pelt them with garbage.

Several men burst out of the White mob, break through the barricades, and make a dash for the entrance. Pointing their guns, the cops bark orders: "Freeze! Get down on the ground!" Faced with the barrel of an automatic, the wannabe heroes cannot help but comply. The cops hold them down and cuff them.

Someone throws a rock at the cops. Someone else hurls a bottle. It shatters against a shield in a shower of glass.

★

Amidst the bustling cops, Reggie stands frozen, his quivering eyes fixed on Tom's still face. Ray comes up to him and takes him by the shoulder: "C'mon, let's get you outta here." He starts to lead Reggie away.

Abruptly Reggie yanks his arm free and recoils: "No! No. I gotta do something. I gotta fix this." He looks up at Ray: "Turn it back on. Please."

The cops stop what they are doing and look at him.

Reggie gazes at Ray, silently pleading. Ray wavers. Something in Reggie's voice and manner persuades him to consent. He shakes his head and sighs: "How much worse can it get?"

He grabs the walkie-talkie: "Mikey, turn it back on."

★

The White, Black, and Mestizo mobs hurl debris and curses at the riot cops, who strain to keep the mobs away from the building and each other. Linda shouts commands as rocks and bottles crash against the shields.

Furious men fling rocks at the radio station, denting cars and smashing windows, while others vent their rage on nearby buildings and vehicles, ravaging the street.

A group of White men roll over the SWAT truck, douse it with gasoline, and set it on fire.

The cops struggle to hold the barricades against the rising onslaught as a full-blown riot threatens to engulf the city.

★

The lights come back on with a thrum. Reggie staggers to the console. Sits down at the microphone. As the surprised cops stare, he takes a deep breath, swallows hard, and begins:

"This is Reggie Miles... There was a... a terrible accident... Tom is gone."

A scattering of people in the raging crowd stop and turn to listen.

"I'm sorry. I didn't want this. I think he was a good man... a family man."

Ray looks down, frowning.

"I didn't..." Reggie searches for words. "I just wanted to help my people."

Outside, more people stop and listen. Men and women in the three mobs turn on and turn up their radios.

"But I see… what I'm seeing is… it's bigger than that. It's about all of us now."

A brawny Black youth pulls a Molotov cocktail out of his sweatshirt, flicks on a lighter, and is about to set the cloth wick ablaze when a friend puts a hand on his arm and gestures toward his headphones. The youth lowers the Molotov and turns on his portable player.

"Like Tom said, truth and respect," Reggie says. "Truth and respect. We all need it. Every one of us."

Ray, Hector, and the other cops watch Reggie and listen in tense silence.

"Black, White, Latino, Asian, whatever. We all gotta face things as they really are."

Reggie's words spread through the crowd as more and more people stop to listen.

"We all need to love ourselves. Who we are. Where we come from. Love our people. Our race," Reggie says. "Even White people. Especially White people."

★

Colton's fist cuts through the air and smashes into a Black boy's jaw, snapping his head to the side and knocking him out cold.

A few yards away, Sam is on top of another member of André's gang, raining punches. Feeling his opponent go limp, he stops and staggers to his feet.

Smiley kicks the flattened Clam Face over and over. Clam Face stops moving. Smiley steps back, sucking in ragged breaths.

The fight is over. André's gang lies scattered on the ground, battered, bloody, and barely conscious. Colton's gang stands over them, looking almost as torn up as their enemies, breathing heavily, still churning with adrenaline.

Colton, his eye bruised, his mouth gashed, looks over his beaten adversaries. Sees Zero twitch.

He grabs Zero by the hair and lifts his head, making him yelp in pain. "Who's your leader?"

No answer.

Colton pulls harder.

Cringing, Zero points a trembling hand toward André.

Colton lets go. He rises and steps toward André, who is trying to crawl away, his mangled arm trailing blood.

Eyes afire, Colton slowly raises his .44 Magnum, aiming at André's head. André writhes on the ground, desperately struggling to escape, his face filled with panic. Colton eyes him with revulsion. No mercy.

"Wait!"

The frightened voice makes Colton stop and turn.

Odette – the girl from Billy's school – stands at the edge of the playground, wide-eyed and trembling.

As the gang watches intently, she cautiously steps to the boombox on the spring rider, keeping her eyes on Colton and his gun. She turns it on. Reggie's voice crackles from the speakers:

"…each other. All of us. White people… White Americans… we aren't enemies. We don't hate you. We just gotta… fix things. Heal ourselves. We're grateful for your help. What you've done for us. And we respect you."

Colton and his gang listen, moved by Reggie's sentiment and sincerity despite themselves, their anger fading.

"Enough," Colton says.

Startled, Odette kills the radio.

Colton looks down at the maimed André, who stares up at him, aghast. "Next time, you're dead." He turns and trudges away, followed by his gang, as Odette stares after them.

★

"…We don't have to be friends or work together or live together – but we do have to respect each other. We have to stay human. 'Cause we're *all* human," says Reggie, his voice growing stronger. "We all got that holy spark. The spirit inside us. And we all need to see that."

Amidst the silent cops, Ray and Hector look at each other.

"It's the only way this is ever gonna work. We can all make the choice – to treat each other with respect. No matter who you are. No matter your race or creed or gender or how much money you got. Respect."

The riot has come to a halt, and the somber crowd listens to the broadcast as police sirens wail in the distance.

"Even if you can't stand them, want nothing to do with them. Even if they hurt you. Respect."

In the Milton high school cafeteria, students of all races listen on their players, smartphones, and tablets.

"Respect for each other's race. Each other's hoods. Communities. Respect each other's women. And men. Respect each other's stuff. Each other's money. Don't take more than you give."

In homes and offices, restaurants and bars all around the city, people listen in, forgetting their cares, caught up in Reggie's fervent plea.

"We gotta let each other be. Let each other be free. Respect each other's freedom."

In the intensive care unit of the county hospital, a nurse discreetly listens on her smartphone as Billy lies in his bunk, bandaged and still, his heart rate monitor pulsing with a steady beat.

"It's the only way. *Respect*."

Reggie's heartfelt broadcast soars over the city, across the state, all through the country, and beyond.

"And who knows, maybe someday we'll even get to love."

Under the starry sky flows a river of candlelight. White people carrying candles stream down the streets, converging on the KYLX radio station, which has become a place of legend – the epicenter of the White Awakening. They come with their spouses, their parents, their children. They come to be with their own and to remember what must never again be forgotten. They come to honor the man who gave his life to unite them.

A lot has changed in the last seven years. The National Association for the Defense of European Americans, or NADEA for short, has arisen to guard and fight for the rights of Whites. The White Voice has become a major force in the media. The Supreme Court has affirmed Freedom of Association in all its forms as a basic human right, striking down law after law.

But the most powerful change has been in the minds of the people. Bit by bit, Whites woke up to primal truths and rediscovered each other, remembering who they are – one tribe with shared genes and memes, ways of being and ways of loving. They stopped apologizing for the sins that they themselves did not commit, stopped pandering to the other races, stopped letting the other tribes take advantage of them. Shaking off false guilt, they once more took pride in their civilization, the greatest the world has ever seen. White Americans rekindled the bonds of blood with the Whites of Europe and the other continents, gathering up the whole of the White race, united as never before.

It started small. In the wake of Tom Mayland's death, White Americans began to organize in earnest, working together to defend each other and their common interests and rights. A wave of lawsuits curtailed discrimination against Whites in hiring and school admissions. A string of boycotts forced big business to renounce policies that harmed Whites. A network of organizations allowed Whites to join up and help each other succeed. In other words, Whites started doing what every other American tribe had been doing for decades.

But the dark alliance between the richest and the poorest of the world would not go quietly. The would-be masters of the planet continued to plot and scheme and undermine. Continued to spread White guilt and inflame the other races against the Whites. Continued to poison the culture. Continued to chip away at nations. Continued to divert, invert, and subvert.

Only it stopped working. Whites had at last wizened up and built up a resistance to the psychological warfare, the propaganda campaigns, the mind control tricks. Proud citizens stood up to the communist thugs, the legal travesties, the media frenzies. The globalists' stranglehold on the free nations of the world grows weaker day by day. And a brave new tide is swelling.

Despite the histrionics of the corporate media, the White Awakening has largely been peaceful and Nazi-free. Despite all the accusations, prognostications, and denunciations, no race wars erupted, no bloodbaths ensued, and aside from isolated incidents, there was little violence altogether. As Tom Mayland had hoped, the White race united not in hate – but in love.

The crowd around KYLX grows by the moment. A wide-eyed little boy with a candle that looks huge in his small hands gazes up at the windows agleam with candlelight, standing next to a golden-haired family of five and a creased old man holding hands with his granddaughter. But Whites aren't the only ones here. Scattered amidst the crowd are Asian faces, Black faces, Mestizo faces – allies of the White tribe who have come to pay their respects.

For quite a while, the other tribes of America complained ceaselessly and vociferously about the newfound White unity. But when the cries of racism and White supremacy failed to produce the desired effect, they came to realize that it's wiser to ally with a powerful tribe than to provoke it. After all, the Whites did their best to treat the other tribes with respect and compassion, even as they defended their freedoms, rights, and land. And so, bit by bit, the other tribes came around. Some came out of friendship. More came out of respect. Still more came out of necessity.

First came the Ashkenazim. White themselves, the descendants of the Hebrews and the Khazars saw the roiling core of antisemitism in the brown underclass that they had tried to lift up and were scorched by its envy and hatred. Bit by bit, the Ashkenazim came to realize that without the Whites, they would be engulfed by the Third World and their ancient enemies, and Israel would once again be lost to the Jewish people. They remembered too that White America sent her sons to the shores of Normandy to fight and die to save the Jews. And so, the wisest and most grateful of them came to stand with the Whites. They came, and they were welcomed.

Then came the East Asians. Clever and prosperous, the Chinese, Korean, and Japanese Americans saw that they would be the next victims of the envious and angry mob. Bit by bit, the East Asians came to realize that without the Whites, they would be sucked into the

Third World and would lose all they had achieved. Life in America hadn't been perfect, but for many decades now, Whites had been their friends and allies, their teachers, their best customers. Though the East and the West had sometimes been rivals, they had also been sources of precious knowledge to each other. Knowledge and opportunity. And so, the wisest and most grateful of the East Asians came to stand with the Whites. They came, and they were welcomed.

Then came the Mestizos. Many of them first-generation immigrants with memories of life in the Third World, the Latinos saw their neighborhoods descend into crime, poverty, and corruption, becoming more and more like the hellholes they had escaped. Bit by bit, the Mestizos came to realize that without the Whites, there would be no American dream – no liberty, no safety, no hope. And so, the wisest and most grateful of them came to stand with the Whites. They came, and they were welcomed.

Then came the Blacks. The Talented Tenth who wanted opportunities and not handouts. The Christians fed up with the war on their faith. The American patriots. Bit by bit, the Blacks came to realize that without the Whites, they would be forced to contend with the Mestizos, the Asians, and all the other tribes who owed them nothing and wouldn't be nearly as kind as the Whites had been. And so, the wisest and most grateful of them came to stand with the Whites. They came, and they were welcomed.

The other tribes came thereafter, for much the same reasons.

The very last came the globalists. These people, long severed from their roots, had no loyalty to any tribe or nation, race or creed. They saw such loyalties as relics of the past and obstacles to their worldwide pursuit of power and profit – and had nothing but disdain for them. To them, all humans, from London to Beijing to Timbuktu, were interchangeable economic units. But as human nature reasserted its dominion and the tribes tore at the global order, the globalists saw their profits fall and their power crumble. Bit by bit, they came to realize that if they resisted, they would be swept away by the tide. And so, the shrewdest of them acted like they were friends of the Whites all along. But in truth, they came because they had no choice.

For over a century, people of the West had felt misplaced and disconnected, sensing in their bones that something vital had been lost and trying very hard to compensate for it. The people of the twenty-first century have finally figured it out. With the resurgence of tribes, nations, and races came a renewed sense of meaning, purpose, and belonging. Depression, anxiety, addiction, and other mental health problems, so pervasive in the early twenty-first century, dwindle day by day. Drug abuse, suicides, school shootings, and other social ills grow rarer and rarer.

Some welcomed the changes as a long-overdue return to sanity. Others bemoaned them as a return to more primitive times. But no one was especially surprised. After all, tribes have defined human history since its very beginnings and are a fundamental feature of the human species itself.

Whispers travel through the crowd as it parts... A slender figure emerges. Billy's face has taken on the hard lines of manhood. Candlelight glimmers in his dark blue eyes that seem so much older than his twenty-four years.

Standing amidst the crowd, unaware of each other, four men watch him approach the radio station:

Ray Vallero rubs his unshaven cheek and frowns. Caught up in the scandal that followed Tom Mayland's death, he had been pressured to resign from the force but discovered a lucrative career in private security. Widely hated, he keeps a low profile.

Hector Hernandez stands motionless, the sadness in his eyes belying his stern face. After transferring to the Los Angeles Police Department, he has quickly risen through the ranks and is believed by many to be on track to become Chief of Police. He rarely leaves LA.

Jake Hollen gulps and gazes, his hair speckled with gray, his face dripping with guilt and melancholy. After quitting the force, he overcame his disillusionment by teaching crisis negotiation at the Milton Police Academy. He is easily the school's most popular instructor.

Reggie Miles raises his candle into the air, surrounded by his entourage, his face solemn. After his on-air debate with Tom Mayland, his audience mushroomed, and his show has become a cultural phenomenon. He is a living legend.

All four men wish they had made different choices on that sweltering day seven years ago.

Billy comes up to the door, the crowd behind him silent and still. He reaches into his coat and pulls out a white rose. Gently, he sets it down on the ground in front of the radio station. "Miss you, dad," he whispers. Looking around at the faces of his people, he adds, "And you were right – we *are* the world's greatest nation." He gazes up into the stars. All around him, an ocean of candlelight blazes and shimmers, stretching out as far as the eye can see.

Angry White Man is dedicated to:

Jordan Anderson	Jessica Doty-Whitaker	Cannon Hinnant
Laura Anderson	Dorothy Dow	Carissa Horton
Wilma Andersson	Mikel Fetterman	Colleen Hufford
Leslie Baker	Veralicia Figuaroa	Kevin Humes
Veronica Baker	Jonathan Foster	David Jackson
Jason Befort	Nathan Garza	Emily Jones
Greg Biggs	Mark Gassett	Roman Kichigin
Amanda Blackburn	Edward Gentry Jr.	Jordan Land
Norman Bledsoe	Edward Gentry Sr.	Whitney Land
Reese Bowman	Jeremy Gentry	Christopher Lane
Keeley Bunker	Pam Gentry	Randy Lawson
Andrea Camps	Steven Gibbons	David Lenox
Robin Carre	Anna Gilvis	Chandra Levy
Channon Christian	Darren Goforth	Tommie Lindh
Rosalie Cook	Fannie Gumbinger	Margery Magill
Jeremy Crane	Sarah Halimi	Tessa Majors
Kyleigh Crane	Karen Harmeyer	Lidia Marino
Melanie Crow	Madison Harris	Paul Marino
Gene Dacus	Zoe Hastings	Wendy Martinez
Justine Damond	Ashley Heberling	Missy McLauchlin
Michael Darby	Brad Heyka	Nichole Merrell

Paul Monchnik	Beth Potter	Dave Stevens
Heather Muller	Zackary Randalls	Christopher Stewart
Daniel Musterman	Walter Reynolds	Josh Stewart
Nancy Nash	Timothy Rice	James Stuhlman
Christopher Newsom	Colleen Ritzer	Angela Summers
Patricia Nibbe	Michael Robb	Mollie Tibbetts
Ethan Nichols	Jake Robel	Barbara Tidwell
Rodney Page	Concetta Russo-Carriero	Willie Tidwell
John Palmer	Aaron Sander	Nathan Trapuzzano
Bobbie Jo Parker	Antonio Santiago	Karina Vetrano
Carl Parker	Amy Savopoulos	Heidi Walker
Charlotte Parker	Phillip Savopoulos	Savannah Walker
Gregory Parker	Savvas Savopoulos	Nick Wall
Autumn Pasquale	Christine Schweiger	Kristyn Warneke
Karen Pearce	Kevin Shifflett	Brittney Watts
Heather Perry	John Shockley	John Weed
Norma Petrash	Nettie Spencer	Joyce Whaley
Patric Phillips	Logan Stacks	Tyler Wingate
Dana Pliakas	Kate Steinle	Raymond Wood

and countless other men, women, and children whose murders were hidden from the public in the name of political correctness.

Pass it on ;)

Made in United States
North Haven, CT
11 July 2022

21212654R00129